A REVERIE OF ROSES

THEA HAWTHORNE

A note from the author

A Reverie of Roses is a cosy sapphic fantasy romance with low stakes and low angst. It contains one fade-to-black scene, some adult language, and suggestive description.

This novella uses Australian/UK English spelling and conventions, which may differ slightly from those familiar to US readers.

It is the second interconnected standalone in the *Muses of Esk* series. If you'd like to find out more about the world of Esk and stories within it, join my newsletter list here:

www.theahawthorne.com/newsletter

HERON'S REST
an
incomplete map
of the gardens
& surrounds

Chapter One

She doesn't mean to say it.

She knows it's going to be a problem as soon as it's out of her mouth. Her friends are staring at her like she's just thrown sand over their paint palettes.

I can paint anyone and anything, and do it a good sight better than you lot.

It should have stayed in her head, silent. But she's gone and said it, and now it's too late. They've both heard it. She takes a sip of her thyme-water and tries to look like she meant it. *Good going, Nora.*

"Anything?" Emlyn says, leaning closer. "That's quite a claim for an artist like you."

She bristles. "And what do you mean by that?"

His handsome smile does nothing to soothe her. "I only mean that you've been having a rubbish year. Maybe you need to take a break from it all. Go to the countryside."

"No, thank you. There's nothing but leaves and lichen out there."

"At least a landscape won't run away from you," mutters Juniper.

The back of her neck burns. She sips her drink again and refuses to look away from their amusement. Juniper and Emlyn are Nora's closest acquaintances, and also her biggest rivals. They are both dressed in evening wear, having just returned from a dinner party with a more illustrious friend. She doesn't know why they've stopped by her townhouse, other than to rub her face in the fact she hadn't been invited. They're draped over the worn sofa by the window, pretending to be far finer people than they are, and they're looking at her in a judging fashion.

Her portrait subjects *do* run from her. They tell her she stares at them too intensely and always looks bitter. She just isn't nice, and, apparently, that puts people off. She hasn't had a portrait client in months, and the last one gave her a scolding on her poor attitude.

Lesson learned. She won't paint a Masey again, anyhow.

Nora's attempts to build a career as a portraitist are not going well, but she needn't these two here, reminding her of it. She is an artist, not a socialite. No one at the academy had told her she had to be pleasant to be a successful painter. People should judge her on her composition and paint-handling, not her niceties.

"Perhaps she can practice her smiles on the rocks and trees," muses Emlyn.

"She can't frighten them, at least."

"Oh, shut it," says Nora. "I'm going perfectly well, thank you. I have plenty of commissions coming up."

"Of course you do." Emlyn pats her arm. "But back to your claim, Bristles. I do feel honour-bound to contest it."

He would, and fairly, too. Her boast had been bluster all through. Emlyn is a good painter. Juniper is excellent. Even if she suspects half of Emlyn's clients only book him for the privilege of staring at his pretty face while he stares at them, it doesn't mean he can't paint.

Still, she's not backing down. "I stand by what I said."

He laughs. "Nora Newell, artist of middling pieces, claims she can *paint anything and anyone,* and do it better than either of us? I really won't let that stand."

"Middling pieces?"

Juniper smiles, drink tipping dangerously in her glass. "You're right, Emlyn. It is quite a claim. Perhaps we should put it to the test?"

"A wager," Emlyn says. He points a finger at Nora. There's paint under his nails, the slob. "You, Nora, will paint a subject of our choosing by the end of summer, and get it into the Annual."

The Annual is the most prestigious exhibition in Esk. The opening of the Gallery is the unofficial start to the Season and any artist fortunate enough to have a painting hanging is assured of a successful year ahead. But it's notoriously exclusive, and so very far above Nora's level. She presses her lips together. "And if I don't?"

"We get your commission book."

Juniper gasps.

Nora feels her face twist. "That's dirty."

He smirks. "It's not a risk, is it? You said you can paint *anything.*"

If she had clients, losing her commission book would be a disaster. It would mean handing over her contacts and customers to be poached. It would mean missing opportunities. It would give an impression she was floundering, having to have her peers pick up her slack. It would ruin her reputation.

"Fine," she snarls. "Just try. I'll paint whatever cursed thing you tell me to paint, and I'll make you all choke on your simpering compliments when it's done."

"Alright," says Emlyn, looking far too content. "I look forward to your commission book. Provided, that is, there is anything in it."

Oh, the *weasel*.

He doesn't want her clients. He must know she hasn't any. He just wants to look at the desolate wasteland of her commission book and feel superior.

"Well? What am I painting?" She knows as soon as she says it, she's given him too much free rein. He might pick someone absurd. He might pick the Crown or her heir, or perhaps Lady Casca or her son. Someone out of Nora's reach, someone untouchable.

Emlyn's golden curls shine in the aetherlight as he casts a look at Juniper, then back to Nora. With great gravitas he says, "You, my darling Bristles, will paint the incomparable Lisette Lacemont."

He's skipped right over untouchable and gone to impossible. Disastrous. Catastrophic.

Lisette Lacemont.

She's doomed.

Chapter Two

Nora stands at the curve of Lightlong Crescent, regretting everything. A faint haze of rain wanders alongside her, just as reluctant to be present as she is. Esk in early summer is muggy, with the weather committing to warmth for a horrid few months before tumbling right back into its usual crisp chill.

It's a frightful time of year, because her mood is always as rotten as the river mud in the roasting reed beds. Especially so when she has to leave her studio. She looks at the letter in her hand. Her curt request to meet with Lisette Lacemont had rewarded her with a date and time, and like some sort of lovelorn social caller, she's here on the dot.

Lacemont. The name is infamous amongst portraitists. Lacemont has tormented artists for years, appearing like a curse to send artists into a spiral of frenzy and doubt. She's a temptation, so Nora doesn't blame any painter for trying. But even the name 'Lacemont' is a hex on the muses. She has never approved any painting of herself. Artists have spent months working only for Lacemont to request the paintings be destroyed. Or she frustrates painters so much they give up, unfinished. Or she disappears halfway through the process, never to return. That is what had happened to Nora.

Fresh from her apprenticeship, Nora had heard the cautionary tales about Lacemont. And yet, when Lacemont had fluttered her lovely lashes at her at an evening party, she'd passed over her card and let the flirtations charm her. She'd cancelled other commissions to make time for her. She'd worn her finest clothes. She'd done everything to impress her.

It had been a learning experience, if nothing else. A lesson to never put so much of herself into a painting again. Never get so taken by a client that it feels personal when they don't come back. Never fall for a sitter.

Nora has kept those lessons close to her heart ever since. She'd have been content to never see Lacemont again in her life. Now, thanks to Emlyn, she is trudging up fancy honey-stone steps to a grand front door, all so she can humiliate herself yet again.

She knocks, pinching the letter so tight the paper creases. The door cracks open, and Lacemont's oval face peeks out. She blinks, as if she doesn't understand who has dared disturbed her.

"Yes?"

"Nora Newell. I wrote." She holds up the letter.

Lacemont pulls the door open. "You did, didn't you?" She steps back, and Nora walks into the snake pit that is Lacemont's personal space. "You're the painter, are you not?"

And that hits, somewhere in her chest. Lacemont is looking at her pleasantly, as if she's a stranger. As if they hadn't spent two very fraught days in almost endless eye contact, once. As if Lacemont had never offered Nora the things she had offered her. *The nerve.*

"I attempt to be, yes," is what she says, hoping none of her thoughts show.

Lacemont closes the door behind her, and the click of the door setting into place sounds very final. The hallway is narrow and arch-roofed, the floor tiled with an overwrought celestial pattern. The wallpaper is patterned with an ostentatious amount of floral ornament. Everything in Lacemont's townhouse is entirely ostentatious.

She clearly follows the *exquisite* aesthetic, as far as style goes. Nora clears her throat and tips her face up. Lacemont glances down at her in amusement.

"The parlour," she says, gesturing to the left.

Lacemont must have been in the middle of something, as there are some folios open on the desk in the parlour, and a half-made list sits to one side. Decorating, perhaps. More fripperies for her extravagant house. Not that Nora can complain too much. It is socialites like Lacemont that keep artisans like Nora going.

"How have the muses been treating you, Nora?" She settles on her sofa. The drape of her body is an invitation, swathed in peach-blossom silk and glowing aether glass.

"They've been neither unkind nor unfair," she says, which is a common and inoffensive reply. She sits, picking a spot as far away from Lacemont as is acceptable.

"You've come to make me a proposition, haven't you?" Lacemont smiles. She's a lovely thing, sharp cheekbones and copper-brown hair, and brown eyes that promise all sorts of trouble. "Oh, do try the biscuits."

Nora takes a biscuit from the waiting tea tray. It's needlessly dainty, jewelled with a precise curl of jam in the centre. "I'd like to paint your portrait."

"You must excuse my memory," she says. "But haven't you tried that already? Whatever happened there?"

So she does remember. Nora is unsure if that is better, or entirely worse. "You never came for the final sitting."

"Oh? How embarrassing." Lacemont's mouth dimples, and Nora thinks she's doing nothing so much as laughing. She pours the tea, then settles back to draping. "I must have forgotten."

"I ruined a perfectly good canvas, trying to sketch you."

"I'm sure you found a use for it."

"Kindling."

She does laugh. "That seems ever so wasteful."

"I didn't want the vengeful, half-finished ghost of *your* likeness haunting whatever I painted next."

"Goodness. I must have a lot of ghosts."

She does. She haunts so very many studios in Esk. So many aspiring portraitists have aspired to her heights, only to fall on the rocks of failure. Nora sips her tea and wonders. Is it the power, then? Is that why she does it? Watching someone bleed out their hope and their hard work, and then letting it all come to nothing. Does it amuse her?

"So," says Lacemont, and her gaze is thorned, catching on Nora and holding fast. "Why do you wish to paint me again?"

Nora swallows, the biscuit dry in her mouth. "I made a wager with some fellow artists."

"How interesting. The terms?"

"I would paint a sitter of their choice."

"And they chose me? Your friends have a cruel humour." She is pleased, though. She shifts, preening in the pretty fall of sunlight from the stained-glass window behind her. "What if I say no?"

"Then I lose."

"Mm." She sips her tea. "Why should I care if you lose or not?"

"You would get a portrait out of it. Of course, there won't be any cost."

"I don't want a portrait," she says, very sweetly. "What else can you offer?"

Nora casts around the parlour, searching for some hint of what Lisette Lacemont might *want*. "What would you take?"

Another little hum over the edge of her cup. She considers Nora, all lowered lashes and gathered mouth. "Perhaps there is nothing you can give me."

That may be true, but Nora isn't about to lose her commission book so easily. "Not so. You are stunning, and it's miserable that there isn't a single portrait of you hanging in any parlour in Esk. Let me change that."

Lacemont raises one perfect brow. She is all artifice. Even now, peering over her cup in interest, she looks like someone's *idea* of interest rather than showing any real curiosity. Had she been so masked the last time Nora had painted her? Yes, Nora thinks. She had. Only Nora had been too naïve to see it then.

"If I had finished my last portrait of you, it would have been something magnificent. It would have been my finest work to date."

"Flattery? I suppose it's working. And? Be honest."

"And I almost despise you for taking the promise of that painting from me." She glances up and catches the finest fracture of shock on Lacemont's face. "I think you owe me."

And *gods*. She hadn't meant to say that. That wasn't flattery. That was an outright insult.

Lacemont puts her cup down, ever so gently. "Owe you? I paid you in full for your work."

"Work you never saw."

"So it is my attention I owe you?"

Nora freezes. "No, I didn't mean—" She sets her jaw. "I don't want your attention."

Lacemont's face has turned into something else again. The pink light falls like petals across her brow, but for a moment, what Nora sees in her face is hunger. Nora has made a study of expressions. All portraitists have. The smiles and half-smiles, the subtle disgust, the anger, the pride. But hunger? That falls with desire, with covetousness, with obsession. She's seen painters look at models with hunger.

She's never had such a look directed at her.

"I get a portrait, you get my attention. Neither things we particularly *want*, but perhaps the venture will be something amusing." The look is gone, melted back into an amiable sort of challenge. "Do you think you can hold my interest until you are done?"

No, Nora thinks. There is nothing about Nora that could hold this beautiful creature's interest for more than a fleeting moment. And so, she will have to make a fleeting moment work. "I will do my best."

"I will accept nothing less."

Nora inclines her head. What has she gone and stepped into? "I appreciate the chance, Miss Lacemont."

Lacemont's soft mouth crinkles, pleased. "Lisette," she says. "You must call me Lisette, if you're going to come summer with me."

"Pardon?"

"I leave for my country house in two days. If you wish to paint me, then I am afraid you shall have to come along with my friends and me. I promise you, we're all lovely people."

The countryside. With Lisette Lacemont and her peers.

Lisette doesn't look away from her, as if enjoying the theatre of expressions that must be running across Nora's face.

"Two days?"

"Well, of course you must come down when you are able. I do know it is short notice." She stands, crossing to her writing desk. There she writes a note and drops it into Nora's lap. "That is the station you will need, and the address of my country house. No need to write ahead. I'll be expecting you by the week's end, at the latest."

Tumult village station, says the paper in elegant, sloping script. Nora's never heard of it, but whatever awaits her at Tumult is going to shape the rest of her year. The rest of her career, perhaps.

Nora hasn't the same shining accolades as Juniper, or the same prestigious apprenticeship as Emlyn. She only has herself, and her work, and whatever glory she can forge from the small chances that come her way. And her chance has come in the shape of a thorn-tipped smile that threatens to sink her if she doesn't impress.

Only Nora has never impressed anyone in her life.

She barely fumbles her way through a farewell, too sunk in dread to be anything other than curt. She stumbles out onto the steps of the townhouse and into the choking shroud of summer rain, the cursed address clutched tight. The paper has Lisette's perfume clinging to it, and by the time Nora gets home, it's clinging to her fingers, too.

Chapter Three

The train shifts off with a rattling whistle, its golden glow lancing through the dim afternoon light. Nora grips her case and steps into the shelter of the station house. Tumult is a sizeable village, a stone's throw from the coast. Nora has never seen the coast, but she thinks she can smell it, even here. A salt-sharp edge to the wind, briny and dangerous. She doesn't like being so close to the coast in summer.

The stationmaster, curly hair pinned tightly under her woollen cap, smiles at Nora when Nora enquires about the address.

"Oh, the manor? Well, there's a path along the river that'll take you just under an hour. Or you might go to the inn and see if anyone might give you a ride over."

Nora decides on the path, and ignoring the woman's dubious look at her two cases, sets off. The briny salt-smell sticks with her along the entire river walk. Not even the summer-mud and stagnant water scent, which she is far more familiar with, can smother it out. By the time the Lacemont manor comes into view, nestled in a flat valley amongst scattered woodland, Nora's hair is slick to her scalp with sweat and she's greatly regretting her decision to walk. The stationmaster might have warned her about the hills.

The path dips down to the valley and throws her back into the tangle of the forest. It's thicker here, and darker than it had been on the hilltop. Thick creepers blanket the ground, eating away at the narrow track. She's so focused on keeping her feet on the path that she is startled by the abrupt end to it.

The clear ground disappears into a thicket of ivy, and her heart plummets. Surely she hasn't come all this way to get lost in the *woods*, of all places. How very predictable for a town-grown woman like herself.

She forges on, trampling across the ivy in her pointy boots, and relief follows, swift and strong. A crumbled arch rises like an island from the sea of ivy, a long-ruined remnant of a wall with a gap where a gate once stood. Beyond it, a rose-choked stately garden beckons.

Lacemont manor. She's not lost. She's come around the back way, is all. Her blouse clings in damp itch against her neck as she hauls her cases over the last of the ivy and through the garden's walls. It must be a vast garden, because she can't catch sight of the manor. Only old walls and tumbled structures, wild-grown poplars and hedge thickets, and ivy over all of it. She picks her way along tilted flagstones, hoping dearly that it isn't too much further to the manor. It's hot, and she's parched right through. The thirst is a pressing thing, and so too are her burning feet, raw and bruised in her boots.

Roses spill over hedges and crumbled walls, and all the shade is scented in sweetness. Courtyards peek from amongst the ivy, some so overgrown she couldn't wade through if she tried. She glimpses an old stone well, tangled right over with roses, and is almost tempted from her path to drink.

But she can't be far off now, and so she forges on. She keeps to the rose-passages, out of the sun, and it isn't long before she passes through a hedge-gate into what must be the kitchen garden. A pair of giant heron statues guard the kitchen door. Even the knocker is shaped like a bird's head.

She raps the knocker, and the door creaks open. A brown-haired man peeks out, looks her over, and ushers her into a homely space. A dusty, patchy sheepdog lifts its head from the hearthstones and wags its tail in silent greeting.

"Lissy said she was expecting one other," the man says. He has a workman's sensible clothes, sleeves pushed high. "Couldn't find the main door, could you?"

"I came the long way around." Nora puts her cases down with relief. The kitchen tiles are patterned with arch-necked birds, and the doorway frame is carved with them.

"Toby Lacemont." He sticks out a hand, and Nora stares at it in shock. She'd heard that sailors and outer-isles folk offered their bare hands as easy as smiles in summer, but she'd never expected to face such a thing herself.

She clears her throat, wishing she hadn't put her cases down. "Nora Newell."

"Ah. Newell." He says this in a dire sort of way, and grins at her refusal to take his welcome. "Apologies. I forget you town folk have odd customs." He claps his palms together, a dull, loud sound in the quiet kitchen. "You'll be wanting to get cleaned up before you join the summer party, no doubt. I'll take you up."

Toby Lacemont, she learns as they go, is the master of the manor and Lisette's cousin. It's a trial for her mind, putting his handshake and common clothes against Lisette's splendour and extravagance.

Lacemont Manor is much like its master. The bricks and stone of it might be grand, but the appearance it gives out is rather world-weary and worn. It's *fine*, of course. A very lovely house. But it's nothing on Lisette's townhouse. In truth, it's nothing on even a middling sort of teahouse in Esk. There's very little art or decoration. The panelled wooden walls have no ornamentations. Rugs line the halls, but they're so faded there's barely any colour left.

Toby offers a few sparse comments as they go, telling her pieces of history she doesn't much care to listen to. And then he ushers her through a door into another part of the house, and suddenly it all makes more sense.

Here are the plush, rich carpets and the paintings and the delicate pottery vases with spilling silk flowers. It's still rather restrained, and under it all, the house is just as old and grim as the rest of it. But finally, Nora feels she is somewhere that Lisette Lacemont won't look entirely out of place.

"Private rooms are through the gallery." Toby leads her along a gallery-style balcony that looks down onto what must be the entrance hall. He takes her up a wide, generous curve of stairs, and into a more intimate, carpeted hall. Soft aether sconces light the way. "Lisette wants you in the Lake rooms, as far as I remember. The yellow door down the end of this hall."

"Thank you, Toby."

He passes her cases to her. "Anytime, Newell. Do make yourself at home. And welcome to Heron's Rest."

Well, that explains all the herons, at least.

The Lake rooms look over the lake, rather predictably. The view is a pretty one, though, framed perfectly in the windows and set off by a deep, cosy window seat. Nora can't wait to curl up with a sketchbook and really sink into the view.

She sits, her feet aching right up through the arches, and lets her eyes flutter shut. The old house is full of sounds. The distant step of Toby, heading back down the stairs. Conversation, floating up from the gardens below. The rattle of tiles on the roof. The creak of the window in the breeze. The river in the distance, the lapping of the lake water.

A laugh, soft and gentle, from right beside her.

She sits up, startled, and sees Lisette Lacemont leaning in the doorway.

"Toby said you'd finally appeared," she says, coming in. She perches on the end of the bed, tipping her smile at Nora as if they are now friends. "Goodness, did you walk?"

Nora tugs at her sleeve cuffs, and turns back to the view. She knows she should say something charming, or friendly. "It's a lovely place."

Lisette is still smiling, though it is not a proper smile. It's the sort of expression that Nora might paint on an idealised market portrait, a hint of shadow and promise of sweetness. Not that anything else about Lisette promises sweetness. She is not even properly dressed, just swathed in a coal-dark morning robe and house slippers, with the impression of a half-together *something* underneath. It is nearly evening, and Nora can't decide whether Lisette is halfway through her change to dinner clothes, or if she's not bothered to get dressed all day.

When she looks back to Lisette's face, Lisette's smile has

deepened. "Is this all you've brought?" She pushes to her feet and goes to investigate Nora's cases. "Where are your painting things?"

"Those are it."

Lisette gives her a curious look. "Then where are your clothes?"

"Also there."

"Gods, Nora. You'll smell like linseed all week long," Lisette says. She flicks the latches and pries open the case. She pulls out a tube and gives it a curious look. "Or perhaps you'll have to wear nothing but your paints. Are there *any* necessities in here?"

"Do you mind?" Nora snatches the tube, placing it back in the precise spot she'd made for it. "These are expensive."

"And your canvas? If it is not to be your body?"

Nora takes a sharp breath. She had forgotten quite how *relentless* Lisette Lacemont is. "My easel and canvases are being ported down from Esk. They should arrive on tomorrow's train. I shall have to arrange—"

"Oh, Toby will go get them," Lisette says, waving a hand. "He likes to be helpful."

Nora wishes Toby was her quarry here, because he would surely make portrait-sitting a breeze.

"I wish to freshen up and change," she says, after a moment. "After which, I will scout a suitable place for painting. I shan't get in the way of your entertainments."

Lisette hums, running her fingers across the neatly packed paints. "I'm sure you won't. Poke about as you please, outside of the private rooms. We haven't any secrets here."

Nora thanks her, far less graciously than she probably

should, and shuts the door on Lisette's velvet heels. The door has a lock. She catches it.

She does have an appropriate amount of clothing, and she puts it away once her paints are all checked and accounted for. A few blouses and skirts, and two finer dresses that will be passable if Lacemont expects her to join in any of the social activities, which she greatly expects she will. She'll be tiresome like that.

Two years ago, Nora had welcomed Lisette Lacemont into her studio, had sat her under a set dressing she had spent three days creating. She had picked the time of day for a particular light, and Lacemont had arrived hours late when the light had turned grey and floodwater dingy. She had worn a different colour than Nora had requested, one that went horribly with the drapes Nora had set up. And Nora had smiled and not said a word, because Lisette had been so *lovely* otherwise, and Nora was already gone on her.

The second sitting had gone better. Lisette had arrived on time, in the colour she was supposed to be wearing, and she had gossiped and charmed the whole time, never silent, and Nora had blushed, and laughed, and volunteered up far too much of herself in reply. Had held nothing back. She had been so eager for the third and final sitting.

She had worked tirelessly in the intervening time, following the ribbons of the muse. The painting had been beautiful, the finest thing Nora had ever painted. She had been *so close* to finishing it, and she wants to crumble away, now, remembering how she had been so eager over Lisette's arrival, like a puppy licking at the hands of its mistress.

And Lisette had not come. Nora's messages remained

unanswered. And weeks later, Lacemont sent a curt note saying she would not be continuing the commission. She paid the price in full, because she was a reputable socialite, but the money did nothing to stem the bleeding of Nora's heart.

Nora had destroyed the painting, of course. She could not bring herself to finish it. To brush at those high cheeks, to push that sultry mouth into a plush, red shape. No. It was better she burned it. She'd have sent herself half mad otherwise.

She thinks she might be suffering some sort of malady, coming back into Lacemont's circles to suffer through the humiliation once more. Curse Emlyn and curse his wagers. Curse Juniper and her sharp tongue. Curse herself for falling for the taunts, and for the wager, and for being here, after all this time, at risk of falling again.

Chapter Four

She stalks the north side of the manor for a painting room. There is a library which she doesn't dare touch, a parlour dressed in faded florals which would need too much rearranging, and then, like a fortune-favour, a forgotten side-room. It's blessedly sparse. The late sunlight seeps through dusty glass, glazing the room in gold. Warmth soaks through everything, deepening the threadbare upholstery and the dark wood. The decoration is a century out of date, restrained and faded, and Nora marvels at the wallpaper, a simple design so empty and spare that it puts her in the mind of a blank canvas prepared for work.

The main furniture is a rather lovely cream sofa with an ornately carved frame, and a matching footstool, and a crooked card table. There is an abandoned trolley-table that she hauls out of a corner. It will make a decent painting table.

"Ah, so this is your spot." Toby is in the doorway, looking around with approval. "A fair hideaway from the fuss."

"Do they all descend on you every year?" she says, crouching to begin rolling the large carpet to one side.

Toby comes to assist her, and together they handle the dusty thing out of harm's way.

"The crowd changes, year-to-year. Underwood has come a few times. Felix is the only one who visits often. The rest, well. It depends on Lissy's fancies, doesn't it?"

A lot depends on Lisette's fancies, would be Nora's guess.

"Do you need anything else to set up? There's a fair bit of old furniture around this place."

Nora fills him in on the imminent delivery of her equipment, and after a bit of further discussion, he agrees to collect it. He also promises to find her a stool for when she tires of standing. "Thank you," she says, dusting her hands off on her skirt. "You are a kind host."

"Hah. Don't catch me up in hosting duties. That's Lissy's business alone." He gives her a nod. "She's never brought a painter before, though. Doesn't tend to like them."

"I'd rather gotten that impression, yes."

He laughs. "Don't let her prickle you too much. She enjoys being a chore." He points down the hall. "The stone gallery is down there. There's an old collection of paintings, if you are at all interested."

By the time she's marked out the best position for her easel, and dragged her requisitioned table into place, the dinner bell has rung. It has the chaotic jangle of a hand-rung bell, and rung with enough enthusiasm that she'd wager a year's income on it not being Toby ringing it. Regardless, she ignores it. She isn't here to make nice with Lacemont and her no-doubt equally tiresome friends.

She goes to the stone gallery instead. Bare stone walls reach for vaulted ceilings, forging an echoing space that makes music of her footsteps. On one wall, windows look out over those strange, forest-drowned gardens. On the other are the paintings. A century older or more, and needing a fresh coat of varnish and some careful attention, they mostly depict neat groupings of past Lacemont family members in the landscape. More often than not, the figures sit by a well. It is, she thinks, the well she glimpsed in the gardens. It is a quaint thing in the pictures, the rough-hewn stone turned into something tame and charming.

"It's a wishing well," says a soft voice in her ear.

Nora flinches and takes a good step back. Lisette gives her a warm smile.

"It's older than the house, and the water it gives is still clear and good. You should try it while you're here."

Nora hadn't heard her approach at all. There must be a trick to not making the gallery sing. "So it's just a regular well."

"I suppose it might be, if you didn't make a wish," Lisette says. She's dressed in a loose gown of seashell pink, with a gold and pearl necklace looped lazily around her pale neck. Nora wants to trace the curve of that neck with her paintbrush, echo the gentle slope of her shoulder with paint. Tease that faint flush of her lips with glowing vermilion.

She doesn't even *like* vermilion. It is too loud, too bold, too full of angry life. When it is on her palette, it steals her attention from her other paints. It stains every mix it enters, wrenching all the colours in its own direction. And it's expensive, and she loathes spending money on something that makes her feel so dull. She glances up to see Lisette watching every track of her gaze.

"I do suggest you make a wish," she adds, and Nora has to drag her thoughts back to the conversation. "It might be put out otherwise."

"I think I'm beyond wishes."

"Ah, only hard work and raw talent for you, then." Lisette holds out her arm in invitation. "The rest of us must make do with the fates' fancies. Will you accompany me to dinner?"

She is trapped by that arm, and Lisette's promise of a smile, and those brown eyes. It's as pretty as a mask, and she's sure that's all it is. Lisette's play-act of manners and niceties. "If I must."

"You must."

And so Nora does. The dining party is in a small room on the first floor. Tall, panelled windows lead out onto a stone balcony, barely wide enough for a person to stand. The land-scape slopes away into the night, a velvet-and-ribbon tangle of deep greens and evening blues, the last gilding sunlight setting the edges of every tree alight like festival lanterns. The sky reaches forwards, blanketing the distance in hazy clouds, and the lake is a glass-white brush mark through the woods. It's almost as pretty as Lisette had been standing in the gallery.

It takes her a few beats too long to realise the room is waiting on her, conversation falling into silence. The dining table shimmers with little aetherlights crafted to look like candles, placed amongst plates with baked fish and summer fruits and simmered vegetables. The scent catches in her stom-ach, makes it twist in hunger.

"Nora Newell," says Lacemont, voice ringing down the table. "A painter."

This is met with a ripple of murmurs and a handful of pleasant faces. There are four people at the table, though none of them are Toby. He must be eating elsewhere. Nora envies him.

A woman with rich, dark hair bundled up in an ivory ribbon smiles at her. "Not trying to capture our Lissy, are you?"

The person beside her takes a pointed sip of wine. "Greater hands have tried and failed."

"She doesn't like being pinned down," says another. He gives Lisette a playful smirk. "Not by obligation, or paint, or anything else, either."

"Certainly not by you," returns Lisette, good-natured. She gestures Nora to an empty seat. "I've better places to be than beneath you."

He laughs, and the table laughs, and Nora slides into the vacant seat and hopes they've forgotten about her already. But no such luck. She's barely started filling her plate when the chatter turns back in her direction.

"So, Nora, tell us about yourself," says the flirtatious man. He spears a piece of parsnip. "I'm Felix Sanderton. I'm an aethergrapher for the Society Papers."

She feels her smile stiffen. Toby's proclaimed regular fixture is a gossip-seller.

"Kalliope," says the woman with dark hair. "I'm an idle socialite, I'm afraid."

"Tyne. A playwright," adds the man down the far end of the group.

The last woman does not introduce herself, because her mouth is full of food. She gives Nora a twitch of a smile instead.

"So?" Felix blinks at her.

"As Lacemont said, I'm a painter." She takes a bite of dinner, and when she's finished chewing, the table is still waiting on her. "I'm here to paint her."

"Of course you are," Kalliope says, talking right over whatever Felix had been about to say. "Which atelier did you apprentice in? Would we have seen your work anywhere?"

She picks apart a piece of artichoke with her fork. "I shouldn't think so. I mainly work in private commissions. My apprenticeship was with Marget."

"I haven't heard of them."

Nora isn't surprised. Percy Marget isn't a well-known name in Esk, though most would have seen his work about. He's a quiet sort of painter who runs a decent trade in painting idealised portraits of popular figures—airship captains and gunners, well-known socialites, the heirs—and selling them at the markets. Nora had spent a large portion of her apprenticeship painting increasingly improbable portraits of Admiral Fairthorne, copying the same aethergraph over and over. Emlyn never lets her forget it, either. Juniper has one such portrait hanging in her parlour. Both those wretches revel in her humiliation.

"He's a market painter." She smiles politely at Kalliope's surprise.

"Oh," she says. "How interesting."

"You could paint each of us in the style of a market painting," Felix says, sounding far too excited at the idea.

"She's here to paint me." Lisette's tone brooks no argument. "Leave off my painter, Felix."

"Come on, Nora." Felix leans over the table, his sleeve dangerously close to his plate. "Surely I'm a more interesting prospect than Lissy. Look, I have an excellent jaw."

"I can do an exceedingly wanton look," chirps Kalliope, and demonstrates. She's entirely honest in her claim.

"I could pose as any stage character you desired," Tyne says. "Really, we're all an artist could want."

The other woman, who has a pretty silk scarf tied around her throat, snorts. "All an artist could want to avoid, perhaps. You'd never sit still."

She's drowned in a chorus of objections, and when silence falls again, they all stare at Nora.

All Nora can think to say is, "No, I don't think so."

It's the wrong thing. She stares at her plate as silence hangs.

"Well," Felix says. "That's rather rude." He turns and snatches the conversation away from her then, and though she supposes that means he deemed her insufferable, she's grateful to be overlooked.

Well, not entirely overlooked. When she glances up, Lisette is watching her, the rim of her wine glass resting against her smile.

Chapter Five

The next day, Toby takes the cart and farm horse to the station and returns with her canvases, her easel, and a further case of supplies. He places them in her chosen room with the air of a man handling a dangerous creature, and escapes before she can think to thank him. Clearly, Toby Lacemont has gotten none of the charm but all the kindness in the family.

Setting up her painting space settles something inside her. It soothes the raw-edged anxiousness that has been growing, and she lulls into the easy dance of the routine. Adjusting her easel. Tightening the canvas. Laying out her palette and preparing the ground.

She goes for her usual technique of a warm, earthy terra rosa. Lisette is all warmth, all bronze polish and glowing sunlight. There will be a challenge in capturing that. Last time she painted Lisette, she had been less skilled, less practised. Her ill-fated painting had been good. Excellent, even, but she knows she can do better now.

Nora is not as soft as she had been two years ago. She had thought she'd been painting a charming and kind socialite, the sort of pretty wren that sparkled in dining rooms and danced with nightingales at the Gardens. She knows better now. Lisette is no charming wren. She is a harpy, waiting for a pitiful feast to be laid out beneath her.

She must be, to so easily have torn out Nora's heart without a thought. *Artistically* torn out her heart, of course. Nora's heart was for her art, and her art only. It did not ache for petalled lips and promising smiles. It did not get bruised by a curt dismissal. It did not sting for a year or more with the memory of it.

The door rattles behind her, stiff on its hinges. She doesn't look up from her work, carefully decanting an extra measure of walnut oil.

"You're late," she says.

There is a whisper of silk. Nora looks up and watches, half-stunned, as Lisette drifts across the room in a dazzling master-work of a blossom-pink gown. It almost moves like petals in the wind, weightlessly. However can she paint that movement?

Lisette turns a slow circle, taking in the room. Nora has rearranged it some, and moved the cream lounge into the centre of the carpet.

"You wish to have me here?" Lisette says, casting a half-lidded look towards her. Her fingers brush the back of the lounge.

Nora swallows. She bundles up the drape she has pilfered from upstairs. "Yes, and you mustn't move. The light is good, there, and I'd hate to lose it."

"Understandable." She melts across the sofa, one arm carelessly resting along the edge, her body reclined as if she is in the middle of a particularly indulgent nap. Her chin is tipped back, her neck a long, pale line. Her chest, gracefully held by her boned chemise, is a rapture of gentle light, scattered lily-honey-aurum.

Nora drapes the fabric over the back of the sofa, tucking it under Lisette's ankles so it frames the gentle shape of her. Lisette moves her legs obligingly at Nora's touch, and that's dangerous too, the way Lisette keeps her half-lidded gaze on her as she follows Nora's lead.

"There," Nora says, snatching her fingers back. They feel as if they've been scalded, though they've touched nothing warmer than silk and stockings.

Lisette is unaffected. "The weather is lovely today. We're planning to take a ramble through the forest after lunch. Will you come?"

"I'd rather paint."

"Well, you might paint out of doors, too."

"I don't paint in such a style." She escapes back to her painting table to hide behind her sketchbook. "I'll leave that to the open-air enthusiasts and their attachment to absurd hats."

Lisette laughs, like it had been a joke. If she had ever *met* an open-air enthusiast, she'd know Nora was deathly serious, both about the sort of character one needed for the open-air, and for their hats. Emlyn and Juniper both participate in open-air painting sojourns, which is all Nora needs to know to avoid them.

Hypocrites. They had mocked the idea of her painting landscapes, when they spent so much time soaked to the neck in them. She wrenches her thoughts back to the task at hand to find her thoughts taking shape in her sketchbook without her conscious attention. Her charcoal dances beneath her fingers, eager to become Lisette's soft hair and drifting silk. And when the sketches are done, she picks up her brush.

Nora takes up a dab of umber, considering Lisette. It is a beautiful pose. It is a touch daring for the Annual, especially with the way Lisette's gown slips from her shoulder, and the way the shadow pools, inviting and madder-dark, between her breasts.

But here, now, in this light, in this room, Nora couldn't care less for the Annual. Her brush is moving, tracing the lines of that shape. Of Lisette. Coveting her, *wanting* her, in the way Nora only ever wants when she is painting.

For a small, intoxicating space of time, Lisette belongs to Nora.

Then Lisette's lips part and her acorn-brown gaze rests on Nora. "So, Nora," she says. It's a whisper, as if she doesn't wish to disturb. Which clearly she does, or she would not have spoken. "What do you think of when you paint?"

"Mostly I am hoping my subject is not about to do something so unpleasant as speak." She nudges a paint stroke into place with her thumb.

Lisette's mouth twitches. Nora notices, because she is trying to sketch it in, and the movement irritates her. "I am a disappointing subject, then."

"You haven't been sitting long enough to disappoint me yet."

"No? And how long will I have to strive for, to be counted as disappointing?"

"At your current rate, another half-second should do it."

She stabs at the canvas, and smiles. The mark lands right, and it feels like a victory. "No, don't talk anymore. It doesn't add anything to the prospect."

"I remember you being a fair bit more amiable," Lisette mutters, but she settles.

Amiable, perhaps, because she'd been infatuated with the beautiful woman who had sought out her talents. Nora had been trying to impress her. Now, Nora knows that there is nothing to be won in impressing Lisette. She only needs her to be a willing subject, preferably a *silent* willing subject.

And she is, for a while, until she yawns, and the movement shifts her entire body. Nora can't help the hiss of frustration that cuts from her lips.

"Surely you've been at it long enough," Lisette says. "Take a break. Come, talk to me."

Nora sets her brushes aside and steps back. It is not a bad time to take a rest. The forms are there, and the light too. She'll have to let the underpainting dry before she goes in with colour, and that'll take a few days. She prefers to finish a painting in no more than two sittings, maybe three, so as to best capture the life and presence of the sitter.

The presence of the sitter is currently very loud, coaxing Nora over by calling her name, drawing it out like honey from a spoon. "Come, Nora. You cannot stare at me with such hunger for *hours* and then not even share a handful of words with me."

Nora's grip fumbles and she barely catches her bottle of walnut oil. "Hunger? What nonsense is that?"

"I am a perfectly delectable prospect, I'm sure. If I was a

painter, I would delight in painting me." Lisette's mouth dimples in amusement.

Nora ignores her and continues cleaning her brushes.

Lisette clicks her tongue. "So taciturn. You know, I've been sitting here all morning thinking about your lovely studio in Esk, with those interesting curtains. Do you still have it?"

"I do. Though I do not think my curtains are at all interesting."

"Well, perhaps not. I confess, I wasn't really remembering your curtains. I was remembering the way you looked at me when you thought I wasn't watching."

Curse her. Nora wipes the brushes on a rag. "Perhaps the light was poor, and I was straining to see."

"No, I don't think so. Were you a little caught on me? You'd hardly be the first."

"Nor the last, I shouldn't think." She packs her palette into the keep-box that will keep the dust from the paint.

"I didn't mind. I liked the way the light caught in your eyes when you were concentrating. It still does it, you know. Even now, as you are concentrating so hard on not listening to me."

Nora, having nothing more to do at her painting table, comes to unpin the drape from where she had tangled it around Lisette's legs. "Hold still."

Lisette does. "Oh, very well. No fond reminisces, then?"

"What I remember most fondly is how little you spoke. Where did that go, I wonder?"

She doesn't expect Lisette's laughter. Maybe she should have, and maybe she should have prepared herself against it, because it slips right through her defences. It's a laugh like a rustle of a hundred bird wings in flight. Gentle, and vast in its promise.

"Ah, now she plays. You were very charming at dinner last night. I think my friends all rather liked you."

"Your honesty is as absent as your silence." Nora bundles the drape and takes it to sit out of the way. She got most of the form and shadow on the canvas, so it will not matter so much if it doesn't fall in the same way for the next sitting. The folds of Lisette's dress, however, will have to be arranged carefully.

"But my charm makes up for them both." There is the threat of laughter in her voice again.

"We're done here," Nora says, and refuses to look up at the whisper of silk. When she next turns around, Lisette is gone.

Chapter Six

*W*ere you a little caught on me?

How dare she ask Nora that? Dredging up the indignities of their past is rude to the point of insult, and Nora fumes about it through a stilted dinner, and right through to the next day.

When Lisette invites everyone to play parlour games in the long room, Nora escapes to the gardens. She would rather eat her toxic paints than play an hour of Flirtation with that lot. It's not that they aren't friendly, because they are. But Nora can't shake the feeling that they are friendly in the same way Lisette is friendly. As a mask, an act, an amusement.

They make everything they do an amusement, whether it's ringing the dinner bell or playing cards. She's at a loss to understand what they do with their time, otherwise. So far, she's seen a great deal of talking and strolling in the half-wild gardens, and at least one of the assembly has some talent in music, because she hears a piano sometimes, often accompanied by singing.

They fill their days with nothing but each other's company. And even Nora cannot deny there is something tranquil in the way they sometimes fall silent, draped across the parlour with barely a gap between them all, and spend an hour in drifting peace. She has never witnessed anything like it. She enjoys her own social circles well enough, but with artisans, the time is forever filled with gentle boasting and challenges. It is exhausting. It certainly isn't tranquil.

She pushes aside an ivy curtain to cut down a damp path. The leaves shiver water over her head, cold creeping down her neck. She wipes them away, irritated at the rain, and the gardens, and her own thoughts.

Maybe her poor view of friendship is only because she is forever choosing to spend time with people she measures herself against. Even every lover she's ever had has been an artisan of some sort, and Nora could never figure out how to celebrate their achievements without feeling sour about her own. Others have figured it out, she knows. Artemisia and Finch are going along quite happily together, somehow working to create marvels greater than anything either did alone.

She tries not to feel sour about that, either. If Arte could see such potential in Finch's work, why had she never seen it in Nora's?

She thwacks away a grasping tendril of thorn-tipped rose vine. The gardens are deep here, swallowed by the reaching woods. Toby clearly doesn't mind the intrusion, for there is little being done to prevent it. Stone walls, once marking neat passages and courtyards, are drowning in a flood of emerald and viridian. It makes for a deep, luminous riot of green that she's tempted to paint, though she's certain her skill isn't enough to capture it.

The passage opens up into a wind-strewn glade surrounded by birches. White roses spill over what might have been a wall once, but now is just a pillowy effusion of sweet blossoms.

"Afternoon," says a voice, and Nora near jumps from her boots. Toby sticks his head from around the roses, his dog at his feet. He has calf-skin gloves up to his elbows and a nasty-looking pair of shears. "Searching for the wishing well, are you?"

Nora swallows back her initial reaction, which was a heartfelt curse. The well is as good a destination as any, so she nods. "Lisette rather made a deal of it."

Toby smiles. It's a fond look. "Well, she would. We all make a fuss of it. It's like family." He gestures with his shears. "You're almost there. Good work on navigating that maze."

He leads her through another crumbled arch, down a twist of hedged path, and then the way opens into the rose-shaded courtyard. The well sits a few paces away, looking far more crumbled and tired than it had in any of the paintings. She approaches it, leaning on the edge to peer into the depths. The stones shift beneath her palms and she jerks backwards.

"Careful," says Toby, too late to be useful. He's got the shears propped in the soil, leaning on them while he watches her. "It's old."

An understatement. It's properly ancient. As old as the bones of Esk, maybe. "Who built it?"

"The family history claims we built it, but that's a load of codswallop, if you ask me. We've only had the manor for a few hundred years. That's a lot older, though you've only my word to go on."

"Has anyone ever come to look at it?"

Toby scrunches his face. His cheeks are pink from his work. "Not that I know of. I haven't delved so far into the family history, mind. There's a load of old journals, but honestly, I found them boring."

"And do you make wishes?"

Toby raises a brow. "No wishes," he says. "Only promises. But that's how I was raised." With that obscure statement, he hefts his shears up. "I'll leave you to it. Come on, Bess."

At his call, a heaping of weeds trembles, and the patchy sheepdog bounds out. She's covered ears-to-tail in mud.

"Ah, Bess," Toby says, suffering. "To the river with us, then."

He goes off, ducking under the ivy arch and into a wilder, deeper part of the garden, his dog tangling at his heels. No wonder the garden is being choked by roses and ivy, if the only gardener to oversee it is Toby, and Toby alone.

She has seen no other attendants around. Lisette and her guests have brought a cook down with them, and they tend to themselves otherwise. Does Toby live in this grand old ruin alone, most of the year?

That's both unsettling and something Nora is a little envious of. To hide away from the world and exist, day-to-day, in the drifting, fading wilderness of this place. Lisette's annual visits might be the only thing anchoring Toby to the rest of the world.

It's only a fancy, though. She saw the bustling village, and she caught the train. They're not alone at the end of the world, here. They're right alongside one of the major arteries of the archipelago, the salt road, that binds humble Coppering to the port town of Alm to the jewel of Esk, and all along it are villages just like Tumult.

When his footsteps have faded, she takes a slow turn around the well, looking at it from all sides. The stone is dark and weather-worn. All the stone in Esk is as honey-gold as aetherlight, and she runs her hands along the strange, charred-bone black of the well in fascination. A few strands of ivy glisten, gem-like, rustling in the breeze. Under the roof, a copper cup hangs on a thin, spooled chain. It chimes, rattled by the wind, but she doesn't drink. The Lacemonts have spooked her with their talk of wishes and promises.

She perches on a lump of stone a short way off and completes a few satisfactory sketches of the well amongst the landscape. And then, because no one is here to know she does it, she draws her pocket-set of watercolours from her pocket and takes a few impressions of the tangled glory of the wild landscape through the far arch of the garden wall.

The air is salt-fresh and brisk. It has her feeling as light as a feather. If she had stayed in Esk, if she hadn't taken that stupid wager, she might be spending her day trying to charm people into her commission books. She misses her studio, misses the peach-gold aetherlight and the dim, grey daylight, and the creaking floorboards marked by years of paint-drops. She doesn't miss the drudgery of it, though. Of accounting her expenditure and balancing it against the worth of her brush marks and her skill.

Get it into the Annual.

Nora has never had a painting accepted to the Gallery's

annual exhibition. Emlyn hasn't either, for all his talent. Of their little group, only Juniper has had that accolade, and only once. To garner the attention of the Gallery is a considerable task. It means showing your work at the right local exhibitions, or getting your work purchased by one of society's favourites, or perhaps doing a commission for a guild or a prestigious institution.

Frankly, it means being sociable and well-liked. Two things Nora has never had much talent at.

But if she can pull off this painting of Lisette, it will eclipse any need to be liked. If she can make the potential of that canvas sing as she thinks it can, the sheer novelty of there finally being a finished portrait of Lisette Lacemont should get people talking. And if people are talking about her painting, they'll be talking about her.

Only to do that, she'll have to avoid the thorny trap of Lisette's flirting. Nora knows her faults. She knows her weaknesses. And she knows that there is an old break in her defences, the exact size and shape of Lisette Lacemont.

Chapter Seven

The moon is a pale milk-glow in the veiled sky, and Nora watches it slowly drown behind cloud after cloud. They're in the parlour off from the dining room, where Lisette's set prefer to spend their evenings, and Nora had not been fast enough to escape being pulled along. She missed her chance, and now she is trapped *socialising*.

A woman sits beside her on the lounge. It is the scarf-wearing woman who had not introduced herself at the first dinner, and has kept silent ever since. She has a graceful movement to her, a way of sitting that makes it seem her blouse and cropped hair are drifting in a slowed fashion. She smiles.

"Clare Underwood," she says, and Nora can't gauge if her smile is friendly or not. "I've been eager to introduce myself. I'm an artisan, of a kind."

Not friendly, then. Nora puts on her most careful face. "Oh? And what is your work?"

"Fabrics," Clare says. "Furnishings and drapery. I design them, and work with the weaving houses."

Nora relaxes. Clare's realm of arts is far enough away from her own that she surely isn't stepping on any toes. "And what do you think of the furnishings of Heron's Rest?"

Clare's laugh is sharp and bright. "As dreary as they are every year. The only thing that changes is that the dust gets thicker."

"Toby got in the dust just for you, Clare," Lisette says, tipping her wine glass in their direction. "I'll let him know you appreciate his good work."

The assemblage laugh. Perhaps this is why Toby avoids them. He's too smart to suffer through being the joke. Clare acknowledges her friend with a flick of a glance, but her focus on Nora is unbroken.

"How did your portrait session come along? Lisette sat the other morning, didn't she?"

The room stills, listening. Nora picks her words carefully. "It's a good start. Lisette is a fine model."

Lisette's mouth is a warning, that gentle curve turned dangerous. "A *fine* model, am I? That is lukewarm praise for someone who stared at me so doe-eyed."

"It was only the light on that beautiful dress of yours that had me doe-eyed," she says, before she can think better of it.

Lisette's fingers twitch around her wineglass. "It is beautiful, isn't it? I have excellent memories in that dress."

There is a ripple of amusement across the room and Nora knows that the joke, whatever it had been, was nothing that included her. The parlour room is airless. The night presses against the window glass, thick and dark, and even the shadows in the corners of the room seem heavy, prowling things. The moon is gone, drowned by the sky.

"Toby said you were at the well today," continues Lisette. "What did you think of it?"

Nora glances around. They're watching her. Felix, and Clare, and Kalliope. "It's a handsome thing. I sketched it."

"I should love to see the sketches," decides Lisette. Then she turns to Felix, and brings up another reminiscence, and the conversation flows on and away in a manner that leaves Nora adrift. An island apart.

She falls to stillness, feeling entirely dismissed. No one makes notice of her or stops her leaving, and she is glad of it. She drifts to her room, moves through her evening wash routine, feeling like she's missed a chance, somehow. She wishes she were home. Socialising has always been a chore, and it's never felt harder than it does now.

Perhaps she should have made a wish at the well. She might have wished for social graces, or a clue as to how to ingratiate herself amongst them. For pretty manners, or a charming humour.

Superstitions are not a thing Nora puts much weight on. She was raised with a healthy respect for the festival observances, with an innate respect for the River Lune and the muses. So even though it's a childish fancy, she thinks she might have made a wish. The well *had* been ancient. The sort of ancient that came with ruined temples and broken roads leading nowhere, the kind of ancient that scholars went all charm-eyed over. She's not superstitious, but she knows that once the archipelago had gods to worship and magic to chase. Perhaps there would be enough of it left in that little well to grant her a paltry wish.

No matter now. One more sitting, and she'll have a

painting done. It might not be the finest painting she's ever done, but it'll be good enough. Good enough to satiate her pride, and perhaps even good enough for the Annual. One more sitting, and she'll find out.

◈

Overnight, the weather turns. Nora's dreams are uneasy, crawling things, where her paint marks bleed through the canvas and disappear, and no matter how hard she works, the canvas is always blank and blameful. She rolls awake, flopping onto her back in the grey storm light of pre-dawn. Her dreams seep away, but the feeling remains — restless and tense.

When she cracks open the window, the salt-stench of the ocean rolls in, thick as cloth against her face. She takes a sharp bite of it, tasting the sea on her tongue. It's a strange scent, unlike anything she's encountered before. Not earthy, and not clean like the scent of winter off the mountains. The wind heaves the treetops of the woods around the manor, and she can easily imagine it as the sound of a rushing river, or perhaps even the ocean itself.

Downstairs, the breakfast room is dark and empty, and so she heads to the other side of the manor and finds the kitchen aglow. Toby sits in a crooked chair by the hearth, boots propped by the fire and caked in mud already. He's smoking a pipe, Bess under his feet. There's a hefty pile of freshly baked blackberry buns on the table, in a wicker basket, and wrapped in linen. Toby must have fetched them from somewhere.

"You've been up early," she says.

"I'm always awake when the house is," he says, a grumble in his voice. "More's the pity."

She steps around the boot prints on the flagstones, heading to the window. "It's been raining?"

"In the night. More on the way, too. Big storm heading in from the ocean."

Outside, the sullen sky skulks low over the wild tangled hedges. "Poor light for painting."

"Ah, well. That's a wrench for you. You'll have to stay until the weather's good again." He considers, then taps his pipe on the stone of the hearth. "Reckon there'll be a bit of sunlight just before noon, though. A last gasp. If you're a quick painter, you might well use it."

"However do you guess that?" The sky gives no hint of any sunshine to come.

"Talent of mine. I'm never wrong." With that curious statement, he goes back to fussing with his pipe.

"Noted. I'll take one of these buns, if I may?"

He waves his hand. "Go ahead. They're for you lot, in any case."

Nora takes two and gets out of his way. She doesn't believe him, not a whit, that there is sunlight on the way, but she also doesn't want to be caught unprepared, just in case it is true. So she sets up, and shakes out the drape, and neatly arranges her paints along her palette.

And Toby is right. The sullen grey blows half-away by mid-morning, a desperate sun sinking through and burning up the mist and rainfall. The light turns thick and golden, and Nora takes a breath of relief.

If it keeps for another couple of hours, it might be enough

to finish her painting. She turns, intending to go fetch Lisette, only to find Lisette coming through the door.

"I thought you might be here," she says. "Shall we make use of this light?"

Nora's surge of gratefulness slams right up against the sight of Lisette. Standing in the doorway. In blue. Her hair, where it had been styled in a graceful arrangement at her neck last time, is piled atop her head. Her jewels are different. And her gown is a sleeker, boned robe in a dark-evening blue velvet.

"What," says Nora, incensed, "is *that*?"

"Isn't it marvellous?" Lisette does a small twirl as she drifts towards the sofa. The velvet shifts like melted wax, as if it is moving across the curves and dips of her body. The skirt is a gathered, plump affair, split down the middle robe-style, so that Lisette's cream silk trousers are on full display, clinging to her soft calves. If she were to lie like —

Well, exactly like she is laying right now, one arm beneath her, one leg pulled up, so that the split runs dangerously high and shows her knee and the curve of some thigh above.

"I can't paint you like that," Nora says. Her heart is thumping oddly.

"No?" Lisette tugs the dress, arranges it more demurely. "Now?"

"Where is the pink dress?"

"I changed my mind. I want the blue dress."

Nora grips her brush so hard the wood creaks. *She changed her gods-cursed mind?* "You want an entirely different painting?"

Lisette has the gall to look politely confused. It's spoiled only by the dip at the corner of her mouth, the threatening of a dimple, that tells Nora she knows exactly what she has done. And she is enjoying having done it.

Nora takes a deep breath. "Go put the pink dress on."

Lisette smiles. "No."

"I refuse to paint you like this."

"Then don't paint me," she says, the warmth dropping from her voice. "Your choice."

She moves, that sinful velvet shifting across her, and Nora starts forwards. "No," she says, the words dropping from her before she means it. "No. Wait." She glances at her palette. She can work with this.

It takes some rummaging through her case to find her precious tube of ultramarine. "Don't make me regret using this," she mutters, as she adds it.

"I'd never let you regret anything," Lisette says, all honey. "How do you like me? Like this? Or shall you come and arrange me to your pleasing?"

Nora doesn't even give her the satisfaction of looking up. She switches a fresh canvas with the half-done pink portrait. Suddenly, it all feels rather too much like her dreams, with the crisp linen of her canvas mocking her. Her chance of escape is gone. There is no way of having a finished work by the end of the day, and she's going to be stuck here for another round of painting.

She wipes in a loose and washy ground, determined to get as far as she can with this portrait in one session. Gods only know, maybe Lisette will show up for the next one in green.

She's not usually decisive enough for the aggressive all-wet method of painting, laying down colours thick and fast and right against one another. It's Emlyn's preferred way of working, and Nora has spent enough time in his studio to have absorbed some of his working method. Something in Lisette's little challenge of a smile has her blood racing, though, and the brush moves like a sword. Like a defence. Like it has a battle to win.

That syrupy light through Lisette's tumbled-up hair. The shifting blue-lilac-black of that velvet dress. And the delicate curl of her smallest finger, pink and pale against the fabric. And the faint flush on her cheek, a touch of carmine, when Nora finally drags her gaze back to her face.

"You look quite fierce today," Lisette says.

Nora sees her mouth make the words. It takes longer for them to trickle in through her mind. "Perhaps because I am feeling fierce."

That makes Lisette's mouth return to the satisfied curl-and-dimple that Nora likes so very much. She cuts it into the paint in deep, tempting pink, then uses a gentle finger to trace the suggestion of that bottom lip, drawing the edge out soft and lost.

Yes, she has gotten the mouth quite right.

Her gaze, next, piercing and brown. Lit up by the light.

Nora is working fast now, because she can see the golden light fading away as the storm comes back across the sky. It is a race, but one Nora is not willing to press any faster, because her painting has reached the delicate stage where the wrong-placed mark will ruin it. The painting is far too much of Lisette for Nora to wish to ruin anything about it.

She paints until the light disappears, smothered by a sudden wash of grey. Lisette clucks her tongue.

"That's that," she says, stretching.

Nora blinks, stepping back. She has kept Lisette sitting far longer than she should ever keep a sitter without a break. She should apologise. But instead, she props the pink canvas against the easel's legs, below the blue one, and steps back.

Lisette in pink is a gentle reverie of elegance. Lisette in blue is a challenging invitation of desire.

"Hm," Lisette says, far too close behind her. "Interesting."

"Interesting?" Nora turns to her. "Is that all you have to say?"

Lisette looks down. She's really a touch too tall to maintain eye contact with comfortably when she's so very close. Nora leans away, unwilling to besmirch that gown with the paint from her hands. And she's very much at risk of that, because all of her is aching to touch.

"They're fine paintings," decides Lisette, in the way one might dismiss a garment design in a catalogue. "Acceptable."

Nora bites back the rising irritation. "You dislike them?"

"From anyone else, perhaps." Lisette leans in, that pink-soft mouth so very close. "From you, Nora? I think I expect a little more."

She cannot think. Her heart is beating too hard, drowning out her thoughts. "How so?"

"The way you watch me," Lisette says, and her voice is quiet beneath the distant rumble of thunder. "Show me what *you* see when you look at me. Because you are painting how I look, but you cannot be painting what you see. No one has ever looked at me the way you look at me. Show me why that is, and perhaps then I'll let you finish."

With that, she sweeps from the room, the velvet rustling in quiet applause, and Nora can do nothing but watch her go, heart trembling in desire and hand trembling in rage. What Nora *sees*? Nora cannot paint what she sees, because what she sees is nothing she wishes to admit to the world. And most of all, she wishes to never admit it to Lisette.

What a joke she would become, to return to Esk with two unfinished paintings and her wager unwon. To slink away from Heron's Rest as a loser. But if the alternative is to let herself be laid entirely bare by her work? Nora will choose to be a loser.

Because Lisette had been right.

Nora paints what Lisette might look like in a mirror. She is not painting what Lisette looks like in her mind. That is too much like a confession of something deep and dark and secret.

Nora might be cow-headed and stubborn, but she is also entirely a coward.

She packs up her paints slowly, wiping her brushes down with care. The twin paintings watch her. Two sets of Lisette's sharp gaze. Two sets of her smiling mouth. She scrapes down her palette and packs it away—if the sun is to be gone for the next day or so, then there won't be anymore painting.

She feels like last night's moon, buried under veil after veil of fog. She will be trapped a few more days in this place and she will have to withstand it.

Chapter Eight

She skips dinner that night. After Lisette and her friends retire to the parlour for reading and games, she creeps to the kitchen. A plate of food has been left out. Stalks of thyme lay across the porcelain plate-cover, spelling out the three strokes of the letter 'N'.

She eats in the kitchen, as rain batters the latched windows and drips down the chimney. Storms are nothing new to her, but there is something about this one that sends her skin prickling every time she catches that sea-scent.

Summer storms can bring terrible things, this close to the ocean. She knows about aetherstorms, about the stormbeasts, has read of them in books and in the papers, but Esk is so far away from all of that. She sees the papers' reports of stormbeasts hunted down and battles won, and reads the list of the dead airguards, too, and listens to the funeral bells toll on the Day of Grievings each year. It's all distant, though. It's not a part of *her* life.

But now? Here, where the sky is low and the scent of the

sea is thicker with each passing hour, it feels closer than she'd like.

Morning brings no relief. She is late downstairs, and the breakfast table is full, Lisette's friends passing around racks of golden toast with merry chatter.

"Nora!" Felix waves her over. "We were just talking about an outing today! The others want to see this well you deemed so handsome."

Nora glances at the sky. It isn't raining, but the night's downpour has turned the gardens into a slick mess of mud and rain-soaked grass. Even the ivy looks rather downtrodden, beaten down by the deluge. "Today?"

He makes a dismissive noise. "What's a little mud? We are in the countryside, after all."

Not everyone at the table appears to agree, but regardless, the plan is made, and Nora is roped in. They are all to walk in the garden after breakfast, and so they do.

Nora tags along after the group, unwilling to walk up amongst their ribald conversation, but unwilling to stray too far into the tangled grounds. They are only a few turns in, and she already feels swallowed by the labyrinth.

Lisette is leading the way, marching them like a festival procession. The ground is slick, churned up by all their feet by the time Nora crosses it, and plastered with dark leaves and windfall. Broken twigs, scattered acorns, green and unripe. An acorn catches under Nora's shoe, and she slips, her ankle crumpling. Clare catches her arm, saving her a very undignified fall. No one is there to catch Felix a moment later, and he hits the mud and laughs so hard he has trouble getting back to his feet.

Nora frowns. It's hard to dislike a man who can laugh at himself so heartily.

"What a day to wear the cream wool," he says, when he's finally helped back to his feet by the combined forces of Lisette and Tyne. "Come on, we can't be far now. Perhaps I can wash my breeches."

"You'll keep your trousers far away from my well," Lisette says, pinching him.

Nora ducks under the wet ivy arch last, and so she sees the lot of them arrayed in the little courtyard. Her hands itch to paint the scene. *That* would be a fitting work for the Annual. They're all in pale cream and almond-blossom, as if there was a dress code that Nora missed, and they look like scattered blossoms over the wind-strewn mess of nature.

At the heart is the well, dark stone glistening with rain. Lisette pats the side like an old friend. "Gather up. Come on, Nora. Whyever are you all the way over there?"

Nora joins them, and there's not a glint of yesterday's challenge in Lisette's expression. Nothing of the way she'd leaned in close enough that Nora might have tucked her palms in the curve of Lisette's waist. Lisette looks at Nora like Nora is nothing remarkable at all, and it is not until this moment that Nora realises Lisette *had* been watching her differently, before.

She had been waiting for something, and Nora has disappointed her.

"Do you drink from it, Lissy?" Kalliope asks, leaning over the lip.

"Sometimes. It's dreadfully cold, though, and my mother always says you should never drink from it if you will not offer it a promise in exchange."

"A promise?" Kalliope gives the depths of the drop a considering look.

"When we were children we'd promise to be good until bedtime, or to help rake the leaves. Those sorts of things. One must always *keep* it, though."

"Sounds like a lark your parents invented to get you to behave," Felix says, and Nora hides her smile behind her palm, because she rather agrees.

Lisette gives him a withering look. "Or you can toss a coin and make a wish. Give, get a wish. Take, make a promise. Your choice."

"I prefer to give," he says, and fossicks a bronze quarter-crown from his pocket. "What's the going rate? I wonder how much value a quarter-crown wish holds?"

He flips the coin in a neat arc, and it slices through the air until it hits the water with a gentle chime.

"I wish for a chance to take an aethergraph of the elusive Casca heir," he decides. He claps his hands. "There. If your wish-well works, Lissy, my career will be made."

"I think you might have needed more than a quarter-crown for that one," she says, rather dryly.

Kalliope is already stepping up to drop her own coin in. "Please grant me more illustrious invitations this Season," she says.

Clare asks for something new and interesting to enter her life, which Nora thinks is inviting trouble, and Tyne asks for a talented actor to cross his path.

Lisette holds her hand out to Felix, who scrounges up another quarter-crown and passes it to her. She kisses it, then lets it fall into the waters. "I wish for delight," she says.

"Delight in what?" Tyne leaps up on one of the fallen stones, balancing there. The creeping roses rustle as he rocks it back and forth. "Details, Lissy."

"Just delight," she says. "The rest is secret."

Clare argues the point, making a decent distraction for Nora. She steps backwards, edging back through the archway. If she stays a moment longer, they might expect her to throw a coin in too, and there is no wish she'd entrust to a mysterious well, or to this lot.

No one follows her, and by the time she's ducked through two arches and twisted her way across a rose-eaten statue garden, she's feeling very lost. Safer, though. It's good to have at least two garden walls between that group and their endless laughter.

She sighs, collapsing back against a weathered stone creature. A hollowed eye peers out underneath an ivy-and-rose-leaf shroud, but there is not enough of it left for her to know what sort of creature it might have been. Either way, it makes a suitable bench as she rests her pounding heart. And then, as her body relaxes, she listens to the rising wind in the roses, and the fading chirps of birds, falling to silence. With her eyes closed, the sounds echo and ripple like a river, until she feels she is adrift in something much larger than a country garden.

It can't be so long that she is sitting, but when she next emerges from her thoughts, the sky is darker. She tips her head back, frowning at the clouds. They're so very close, skimming the tops of the trees, thick as paint swirled across canvas, and the first drops of rain hit her cheek, stinging and cold.

A creeping sensation climbs from her fingers and toes right to her scalp. She knows better than to stay out with the weather changing. Esk's mercurial and at-time violent weather has taught her how to taste the turning of a storm on her tongue. She drags her sleeves down, tucking her fingers into her cuffs.

The summer warmth presses against her skin, cloying and damp. A stir of wind brings a veil of fog and all the garden swirls together. The rattling hiss of the vines and creepers rises like a tide. She hasn't heard the group in a long while.

They've headed back to the manor, then. And so should she.

She hesitates. She is in an old hedged passage, though the hedges are naught by thorny rose-tangles now and the forest has stepped in, saplings and shrubs bursting through the old lattice and stone. Which way had she come? Through that arch, here? Or the other over there? She cannot see through the mist to remember which way had led to the well.

The stone creature watches her with one shadowed eye. The wind rolls through her, colder this time, and the first fringes of rain hit her, sharp and stinging. It'll be mere minutes before the storm sets in properly. She picks a direction and hurries off, boots skidding against the slick stonework. Around a bend, and another.

And then, warmth, colliding with her.

She reels back, grabbing at her obstacle, only to find softness and linen beneath her palms.

"Oh, there you are," Lisette says, voice catching. "Wherever have you been? We went back to the house ages ago."

"Walking."

"Well, how about you walk in the right direction?" Lisette

points off to their right. "Let's go back before we're both lost entirely."

Nora pulls her hand back from Lisette, even as she wishes to grasp her and hold tight. The wind picks up, the ivy shifting and heaving around them like a river in flood. "Your garden is terrifying."

"It's not wise to wander in it," she says, instead of laughing, like Nora thought she might. "Come on."

That's when Nora realises. Lisette's tense face, and the crease of a frown in her brow—she's worried. Whether it's the weather, or Nora's absence, or something else entirely, she's worried.

Lisette turns them around on the path and then hesitates. The tangled roses and the scraggly hedges all hunch and sway in the wind, and the path doesn't look the same as it had a moment ago.

"This way," she says, and drags them through an arch, then stops. A true mist has rolled in, and there is nothing to glimpse ahead but the shape of a wall and the odd, hunching silhouette of a bowing pine.

They're lost as the moon was lost, buried in fog.

Chapter Nine

The mist has them wet-skinned and damp-lashed before the rain starts. Lisette clutches Nora's wrist, her fingers warm in the sudden storm-chill.

"Don't you recognise anything?" Nora asks, as Lisette back-tracks through another overgrown archway.

"It all looks the same," she says, gritting her teeth. "I use the trees to orient myself usually, but I can't see anything over the walls through all this fog."

Nora tips her face to the sky. It's come down to wrap right around them, and as she's gazing up, the clouds unclasp the rain. It falls in an immense shattering of sound. Lisette swears, loud and sharp, as the rain drenches them through. Nora pushes her hair from her eyes and trails Lisette into the shelter of a wall's alcove.

"Toby will come for us," she decides. "He'd never leave me out here."

"Soon, I hope." It's cold, and Nora wraps her arms around

herself. "It's beautiful, though, isn't it? All the mist and the silver rain. It's almost glowing."

"I can't see the beauty in it."

"How can you not?" Nora has never been under a sky like this. The salt-earth-stone richness of the rain as it sluices down her face, the way the sky seems to have swallowed the world. "There's so much movement. The entire world is shaking. How would one even begin to paint that energy?"

"Now? You wish to sit here and paint now?" Lisette's laughter is breathless in disbelief.

"If I had a shelter over my head, and paints in my hand? Yes, of course I would."

Lisette watches her, eyes wide. "Your face, Nora! I see I must face down the very sky itself to be able to bewitch you."

Nora laughs at the absurdity of it. "Perhaps it would make a more obliging sitter for me."

She makes a low noise of disgust. "You are an impossible creature."

"Me? You are the one who wore blue yesterday, just to spite me. You are the most infuriating subject I've had to paint."

"It's hardly my fault if you can only paint what is easy and lifeless."

"*Lifeless*?"

"Aren't all your paintings a little lifeless? I can't fathom why, because there's nothing wrong with your eyes. I *see* you observing. You notice life everywhere, and yet you reflect none of it back."

"Are you an art critic now? Am I to thank you for your thoughts?"

"Perhaps you might just return your own. I keep waiting to hear them, and you give *nothing*. All those polite, prickly manners around my friends, like you can barely stand to be near them. Or is it just me you cannot stand?"

"I like you just fine, Lisette."

"There she goes again with the *fine*. I do not want *fine*, Nora. If I wanted *fine*, I'd have accepted forty portraits by now. I want something more."

"Perhaps none of them attained the grandeur you keep in your head."

Lisette laughs, short and brittle. "I only want someone to see me as I am. *You* do. You *did*. Last time you painted me, you saw me. I know you did. But the paint you put down? An ideal. Lifeless. Not me. Not at all."

"It was a good painting."

"It's not your skill I find lacking. Only your honesty." She turns.

"I paint what I see."

"You paint light and silk, but keep silent on whatever pretty fantasy runs through your head. If you despise me, then paint me like you despise me. If you wish to bed me, then paint me as if you are bedding me. But for all the ancient gods, Nora, don't paint me like I'm just *fine*."

Bed her. Nora does want to bed her. Gods, of course she does. The storm drenches Lisette's blouse to her skin, melted away by the water, the fabric disappearing into the flush of her skin beneath. Nora can see her, most of her, in a way she shouldn't. She looks instead to the dark garden around them, to the heaving skies. If she could paint Lisette now, wet-to-the-skin with her clothes clinging, there would be no doubt how Nora wants her.

Lisette is right, though. Nora wouldn't dare.

"If honesty is what you want, I'll paint you like the headache you are."

"You are such an unpleasant thing without a brush in your hand," snaps Lisette. "I see I have to tie you to your easel to keep you agreeable."

"I'll be more agreeable when you find the right path again. Is this not your manor?"

"It's Toby's and I rarely wander this far. This is your fault."

Before she can answer, there is a bark.

They peer around the alcove, and the patchy sheepdog is there. Bess. She is a diminished thing in the rain, half the width she was with her fur fluffed by the hearth, but her tail is wagging furiously.

"Oh, Bess. Thank the gods."

Lisette hurries forwards, Nora on her heels. Bess trots ahead of them, barking every time she feels they are falling too far behind. The air is wet as lake-water, and Nora can't breathe without breathing in the rain. It leaves her tongue tingling like she's bitten into something astringent. Salt hangs heavy in the wind, leaving her lips tart with the taste of the ocean. She drags her wet hair from her face, blinks through the mist.

The rain has turned Lisette's acorn-brown hair to dark umber and ink. It clings to her flushed cheeks like fallen leaves cling to stone. "We have to hurry," she says. "Now."

Her hand, when she grabs Nora's palm, is a flash of heat and shock. Nora stares at their hands, at the way Lisette twists her fingers between Nora's own, the way they slide together, fitting easily. Neatly.

The last time someone held her hand was...a while ago. Arte, maybe.

"Come on," urges Lisette, and tugs at her.

Nora goes. She trails after Lisette like an unfortunate ribbon tangled up around her wrist. Small, hard acorns pelt them as they pass through a small grove of oaks, Lisette cursing like an airguard at the onslaught. Behind them, a crash tears through the storm noise.

They turn as one. A branch is in jagged pieces across the path behind them, still shaking with the force of its impact.

"*Now*," Lisette says again, and then they are running, Bess circling them and nipping at their heels.

Nora barely stays on her feet. She watches Lisette's boots flash in the mud, kicking up water, and follows. A gate. The kitchen garden. The worn steps to the kitchen door.

And then the storm fades, slammed out by Lisette latching the door fast. The kitchen is warm, a fire roaring, and Nora staggers over to lean against the hearth as she unlaces her boots. She's dripping all over the floor. That's okay, Lisette is, too.

Bess flops down between them and Nora murmurs her thanks to her, crouching to ruffle her fur. The prickling cold of the storm slips from her, leaving a duller, deeper ache of cold instead. "I'm sorry I got myself lost," she says, as Lisette wrings water from her hair. Let out of her bun, it falls to her waist.

Nora has never let her hair get so long. It would make an awful mess, getting into the paints and dragging over her canvas. Still, she envies it as she watches Lisette drag her fingers from her scalp to her ends. Envies it, or perhaps only wants to touch it.

"It's no matter," Lisette says. "I might have noticed you slipping away and warned you, I suppose." She straightens, and there's a wild beauty to her. Her lashes dark and wet, her face pale and cheeks flushed. Her clothes turned to indecency and her hair caressing her temple and cheek like a lover's touch. Her mouth turns up at the corner. "I know that look. You want to paint me."

"Would that be enough honesty for you? To be painted like this?"

She looks almost tempted. "Perhaps. But I'm afraid the promise of a hot bath entices me more. Come, let's see if Toby has the boiler on."

Chapter Ten

The cold of the storm washes off easily, but the strange, stinging sensation stays. It settles under her skin, raising bumps along her arms and making her scalp prickle.

Her small rotation of clothes is almost through, and she knows she'll have to ask how the laundry works soon. She hadn't expected to stay as long as she has. She hesitates before pulling on her knitted jumper. It's the sort of plain thing she wears without thinking, shell-pink with cream roses, but it'll be an eyesore in Lisette's company. Lisette's sort of people never wear knitted jumpers.

She plaits her hair, ties it off in a ribbon, and watches the garden below her window shift into tempestuous shapes and forms. The ivy and trees become heaving waves of shadow, and the wind is thick as a veil, torn through with leaves and dirt. The window rattles.

A low, eerie howl comes from an age away, echoing through the skies. All her body thrums with it. She is a rabbit poised to run before that howl, beating back the sudden pounding of her heart. She's never heard a storm like it. When she ventures downstairs, she finds the others huddled in the parlour. And, for the first time, Toby is there, too. He stands by the fire, hands clasped behind his back.

"Good," he says, when she comes in. "All accounted for, then."

As Nora had expected, there's not another knitted jumper in sight. Lisette, freshly dressed in a pale green draping jacket and almond-cream trousers, beckons her to sit beside her. It's a cosy seat, built for one person to lounge upon, and with two bodies on it, it feels rather full.

"I like this," Lisette decides, tugging at her jumper. "It suits you."

Toby clears his throat. "While the lot of you were bathing and fluttering about upstairs, we had a visitor."

Lisette's attention is stolen. "Who?"

"The local guard-post. It's shaping to be bad weather along the coast, and we're not so far away from it, here."

"A tad more than 'shaping to be'," says Clare. "It fair is."

"It's going to get worse. It may be an aether storm, and the *Tisk* is far enough away that they don't expect it to arrive before the storm makes landfall."

The words blur in Nora's mind. *Aether. Tisk.* She recognises the name of one of the Admiralty airships, the hunting vessels that stalk the summer storms and keep the storms and the vicious beasts spawned within them away from cities.

Nora has grown up amongst aether. She barely notices it most days. It lights the streets and her house and moves the trams and trains and ferries. It is the gentle glow of pretty aetherglass, ornamenting hair clasps and necklaces. In town school, she'd been taught the difference between wild aether, and artisanal aether, and the Crown's potent raw aether, but she had paid little attention. Even at ten, she'd been certain she was going to be a painter. She hadn't thought she'd ever have to know anything more of it than how to paint the peach-soft glow of aetherlight.

The others seem near as rattled as she is. "Would it really reach here?" Felix asks.

"Could do. It's not likely, but the bigger risk is getting flooded in. Either way, don't go wandering in the woods."

"Noted," Felix says, grim. "How exciting, though. A real aetherstorm! You don't mind if I get my gear out, do you? I've never tried taking aethergraphs during an aetherstorm. I hear that all sorts of strange things can happen if there's enough wild aether in the air."

"You know the rules," Lisette says. "Nothing to the papers without permission from all of us."

She punctuates her words with a thoughtful tap against Nora's shoulders, because her arm is slung right around her. When had that happened?

Kalliope sinks into her chair. "Exciting, he says. Trapped here without a gasp of fresh air. And I was *so* looking forward to our boating."

"There's plenty of air in this place." Clare stretches, a picture of repose. "We'll hardly run out."

"Felix is right," Lisette decides. "It's a bit exciting. Like a Starling novel!"

"If it's going to be a Starling novel, leave me well out of it," mutters Toby, and claps his hands together as if to ward off that thought. "Use the house as you will, but stay away from my own quarters. If you get bored, go fossick in the attic. There's always something alarming to find up there." He looks around them all, resigned. "Gods, you are going to be bored, aren't you?"

Tyne sits up. "Consider," he starts, with all the drama Nora expects of a member of the Guild of Theatrical Arts. "We make our own Starling adventure."

Nora looks to Lisette, hoping for some clue in untangling that confounding statement. But Lisette is grinning, all that fearsome energy lighting her up right through.

"I call Starling," she says, jumping to her feet to strike a pose.

"Wait, wait," Felix counters. "Not so fast. I think, when it comes to dashing, rakish characters, there is an obvious choice."

"Lisette," chirps Kalliope, and blows Lisette a kiss.

Clare claps her hands. "A fine idea, Tyne! This will pass the time marvellously."

"Pardon," Nora says. "What are we doing?"

"A play!" calls the group, already acting like a chorus.

"I'm *so* glad you'll join us," Lisette says, tugging her to her feet.

Toby meets Nora's eyes, her alarm mirrored in his face. He smartly escapes. Nora cannot. Lisette is holding her arms too tightly. She wishes she had escaped days ago. She should have packed her cases and trekked back to the train station. If she had, she'd be curled up in her studio on her favourite chair, and maybe she'd read about the storm in the papers and think *oh, how interesting*, and then promptly move on and forget about it.

She would not be here, threatened by a play. Well, a storm and play, but only one of those things is inside the manor with her. Not that the storm isn't trying its best. It's hard to forget about it when it is splintering the sky apart right above her, shaking the stones of the old manor.

Tyne pauses in his antics to frown at the windows. "Do aetherstorms often reach the manor, Lissy?"

"Mother has a story of being locked down for two weeks as a girl, when a storm made landfall. But it's rare. The family has a long history of hunting, though, and there's a very old knife in the library that is said to have been made from beast-bone that my great-great-great aunt harvested herself after a storm."

A poignant silence falls as they all try—and in Nora's case, fail—to imagine Lisette's great-great-great aunt slaying and butchering a wild stormbeast.

"Remarkable," says Felix. "Perhaps Lissy is destined to be our Starling, after all."

A shadowy object collides with the window and they all jump.

"Just a branch," says Clare, after she's taken a brave peek. "We're lucky it didn't break the glass. Why doesn't the manor have shutters?"

"It did. Grandfather had them removed. Said it was an eyesore."

"So if we're all devoured by stormbeasts," Kalliope says, "I'll be sure to blame your grandfather."

Felix claps his hands, rousing their attention back to him. "Until such a fate befalls us, we have work to be getting to. Plays to write, lines to learn, a set to build." He flourishes the door open. "To the attic!"

Chapter Eleven

The storm sets in by morning, and so do the rehearsals. Nora tries to escape, but when she stands in front of her easel, the echo of Lisette's words rattle around her mind. *Lifeless.* She stands there, brush in hand, and doesn't make a single mark. She's still standing there when Kalliope arrives to drag her to the parlour. She can't even claim to be in the middle of anything important, because the canvas betrays her in her blankness.

In the parlour, Tyne smiles at her and gives her a sheaf of letter paper with handwritten stage directions. With trepidation, she sees there are speaking lines. A startled gasp, an exclamation of a beast in the woods, a cry for help, a declaration of gratitude.

"This is your part." He's found a moth-eaten velvet cap, and it's perched askew on his bronze curls. It's irritating how fetching it looks. "You can read them this time through, but try to memorise them."

She glances at the paper again. "Am I the damsel?"

"Oh, very good!" Tyne says, leaning in to fluff up her hair. "You'll have the character down in no time."

Nora takes a steadying breath. He's assigned her the role innocently, she thinks. Even with kindly intentions, perhaps. There are very few lines, and she only has to sit around in the final scene and look imperiled. It's hard not to think of yesterday, though, and the frantic chase through the gardens. The way Lisette had held her hand so tightly and refused to lose her to the storm. *Damsel.* Nora has never been a fretful damsel in her life, and she doesn't intend to start now.

Felix pushes her into her place. "Your lines start on page nine," he says. "Just read, you needn't act."

"I promise you, there is no chance of that," she says, but she finds page nine. And stops. And stares. The assembled players watch her, polite and entreating. She clears her throat. "*You must know what it meant when I could not leave you.*"

A curtain stirs. Lisette, a silk evening capelet thrown across her shoulders, strides towards her. "*And you know what it means, that I came.*" She tosses the capelet aside and clasps Nora's hands. "*I will be gone with the dawn, but the night is ours. Let me leave you sweeter than I found you.*"

Nora chokes on a laugh, startled despite herself. "Pardon. But I'm quite sure I've never read *this* in a Starling book."

Lisette smiles, looking entirely ridiculous in her capelet, and it does wondrous things to her eyes. "We had to invent the dialogue, of course, but after a thorough reading of his latest novel, we're sure this is how that chapter with the maiden on the beach ended."

"I think," Nora says, looking away from the danger of

those eyes, "that you had better run me through the whole scene from the start."

It's a short, amusing piece. She wonders if it's Tyne's work, or if they had all contributed. She can almost imagine them, draped in a carelessly beautiful composition across the sofas, throwing lines back and forth. She'd been harsh to think them nothing but idlers. They have passion, as much as any of her artisan peers, only it's that they aren't trying to *do* anything with it. They simply enjoy it, the way one enjoys sunshine, or rain, or a crisp morning breeze. No aims. No aspirations. No criticisms of their own work, only enjoyment.

She steps up, where Felix is pointing at her, and then stares, aghast, as Felix transforms himself into a hulking beast of a creature with an old fur coat, a horrific mask he's unearthed from somewhere, and the sort of body-acting that she thinks will soak through her nightmares.

"You dance in the festival processions, don't you?" she says, faint.

He tips the mask back and grins at her. "Sure do. Since I was a child. I'm a midwinter wind or a water-dancer, usually."

"Then I must have seen you perform."

"No doubt." He tugs the mask back down and makes a truly terrible wolf-growl. His stalking is better than his mimicry. "Now look terrified."

It's not a difficult role, in the end. They don't seem to need much input from her. The story tracks the brave adventuring troupe on a moonlit night as they save a lost maiden from a hungry pack of wolves, and the first half of the play has Nora sitting on a table doing nothing at all. They don't even make it to her lines, because at the point where one adventurer gets violently torn apart by wolves, Tyne calls the rehearsal to an end. Felix throws the fur coat off with great enthusiasm and demands wine.

She curls up in an armchair, relieved to be spared any further acting. The whole endeavour is a waste of time, of course. That is the point of it. To waste the grey, lightless storm hours, and fill the space with laughter.

"Here." Lisette sits on the arm of Nora's chair, setting a glass in Nora's hand.

Her refusal is on her tongue, but then there's a finger pressed against her lips, stilling her. A flush rises up her neck.

"None of that," Lisette murmurs, leaning in. Her hair tumbles over her shoulder, brushing against Nora's cheek. It smells of roses. "How did the painting go today?"

"It didn't."

Lisette tips her head to the side, a curl of a smile there. "You won't be winning any wagers like that."

"And you won't be winning any opening nights with this play," she says. She means it to be a joke, but it comes out far sharper than she intends.

"I should hope not," Lisette says. "I'd make a poor career of being an actor." She drags her finger along Nora's lips, and then pulls away, going back to pour the rest of the drinks.

Nora stares ferociously at her glass, unwilling to look at anyone else in the room. Her cheeks burn. A poor actor? No, Lisette Lacemont is an *excellent* actor. She is a trifler, and Nora should not let her toy. She should not let her play.

When she drinks, the wine bites at her tongue. It loosens other tongues, too. The conversation flows faster and heavier than the rain outside. Felix drags them through a tale of scandal so sordid that Nora feels it must be true, or otherwise Felix has the makings of a spectacular novelist. Kalliope spins the conversation as neatly as a dancer spinning a partner and brings it around to the coming Season. It's far too early for anything to be known, but still they speculate on the fashions, and the colours, and who will become a notable of society, and who will fall from grace.

"Did you hear?" Kalliope adds, and Nora is barely listening, "Luce's little sister has done work for the Gardens this year."

It hits her like a blow. That lost commission, stolen out from under her, and the memory of Arte across the candlelit crowd, victorious. She lets out a breath, loosens her hand from around her glass. Takes a drink, deep and unwise. Arte deserved the victory, she knows. There's no use being bitter. The right work had been chosen, and that was for the best. She'd have messed it up, anyway, no doubt.

"I suppose we'll all see it before too long," says Felix, as if it is a given that they will all be in attendance at the Gardens once the evening parties of the Wintering Season begin. For them, perhaps it is.

Nora has never been notable enough to warrant an invitation to such events. She doesn't think she ever will. Lisette, on the other hand, looks nothing more than barely intrigued by the prospect. For all her insistence on drinking, she's barely touched her wine. She's primping in a mirror, playing with the collar of her costume, as if trying to figure out how it looks most dashing. "Is she a painter?"

There's a space of silence. Nora glances around. No one is answering. Perhaps no one knows.

"She's a mosaicist," Nora says.

"Oh, well, that's fitting. I suppose she did something for the bathing pavilion."

Clare settles down beside Nora, her wine tipping dangerously in her hand. "Do you bathe, Nora?"

"I've had the fortune of a token twice," Nora says.

"But what good fortune it is when you get one," Clare says in agreement, with the camaraderie of an artisan who understands the weariness of the body and the mind. "You were at the artisan's night this year, were you not? I'm sure I recognised your face from somewhere."

Nora stares at her drink. "I was. My work was not picked up."

Clare clicks her tongue. "Nor was mine. Alas for us both." She says it cheerily, as if it isn't anything so dire. Nora wishes she could be so cavalier about such things, but the rejection had hit her hard.

"So, Nora," Kalliope says, leaning forward in her chair. "How is the portrait coming along? You've been tucked up in that studio of yours all week, and we've yet to see a single masterpiece."

Nora's mouth goes as brittle as summer straw. "I suppose that may be because I have yet to create one."

"Ah, it won't be long," says Clare. "With the way you cast such looks at Liss, your painting must be spectacular indeed."

"Don't tease," drawls Lisette. She's draped across her sofa, slippered feet propped in Felix's lap. If the room was a painting, then Lisette would be the focal point. All eyes drawn to her. "The way she stares at me is almost an art of its own."

The laughter is a bright patter, louder than the rain.

Nora takes another sip of wine. It's sweet, far too sweet for her mood. The shame crawls down her throat, no matter how much she tries to keep the bitterness at bay. Does Lisette truly see her like that? Foolish and gawping at things beyond her reach?

"Oh, don't look so," adds Lisette. "I mean it well. You have a masterful way of handling your brushstrokes." She sips, her smile catching and blazing into life. "I'm sure we'll see finished work some day."

Perhaps they're laughing again. Nora couldn't say. The world has washed out into the thrumming of her blood in her ears. Heat crawls over her. "There you go, being an art critic once more. Perhaps you make a career of *that*."

"I would need to see some art to be critical of," Lisette returns, light as air. "What *do* you call it when you fail to finish a subject, again?"

She's teasing. Nora knows she is. It doesn't stop the wine souring in her stomach. "I call it a failure of the subject to captivate."

The room falls to silence. Her heart is beating as fast as a rabbit in a chase. Lisette's smile fades, and Nora can't look away. The mask, for a moment, is gone, just like it had been gone in the gardens. All she sees is Lisette's sharp, jagged edges, and it is captivating. For the briefest of heartbeats, Lisette has all the danger of the storm.

Chapter Twelve

By morning, the storm has entirely swallowed the world. Beyond the misted glass of her window, there is nothing but shifting, writhing clouds stealing through the garden. Sharp fangs of rain tear up earth, the clawing wind peeling the leaves from the trees.

Nora places her fingers to the cold bite of the window lever. Quietly, so quietly, she pushes down and cracks the window open. Wet, sharp air slices inside, thick with the mulch-salt-brine of an ocean storm. Nora rests her head against the frame and breathes that wild air in deep.

It steals inside her, and she fancies it swallows her like it has swallowed the garden. Wild, fey. Full of fury. There is nothing nice or neat about it. If only she could paint with the same intensity that the storm brings down from the skies!

When she closes the window, her mouth is aching. Her tongue, her teeth. She knows that ache well. *Aether*. She's never seen an aether storm, having spent her life in Esk, but she's heard enough tales from those who have.

With the hum of aether still on her tongue, she skips breakfast and heads to the painting room. It's all greys in the storm light. Watery, unfinished greys, draped in loose, lazing marks. The shape of the sofa, empty. The line of her easel, standing like a leaf-skeleton against the white of the storm. Her painting stool, a dark, anchoring dip of shadow.

They had made no plans for painting, and Lisette might well be distracted with the cursed play, but Nora still tilts her easel to the empty sofa in hope of her.

The storm kills the day, casts night down and leaves her shrouded in it. The light is so constant and dim that it seems no time passes at all. Instead, the hours are marked by the rattling windows and the shadow-dance of the storm-bent trees outside.

Today, at least, Nora finds she can paint. She chases the storm shadows with her brush, pushing the paint into wild and tortured shapes. A reverie of the gardens is forming from her memory, all ivy-green and roses.

The room is shrouded and fluttering—the storm, the light from the flames in the hearth, her brush skipping across the canvas. She paints the way she's always been taught not to. Without care or thought, with the same wild abandon of the storm. She has no destination, only the chase and pull of the process to lead her on. Her sole aetherlight sits on a shelf behind her and bolsters the dim light, the only steady thing in all the room. The storm has seeped into every other thing, even herself. Her bones ache, all her limbs sore as she moves.

But she can still taste the storm on her tongue, and she chases it.

The door creaks and she flinches. Her brush stutters across

the page and leaves a smear of dark umber. No matter, she decides. She'll just work it into the ivy shadows.

"Am I disturbing you?" Lisette is as bright-voiced as ever, but she sounds small beneath the howl of the skies. She's added a tapestried shawl to her outfit, wrapped tightly about her shoulders.

Nora eyes her warily. There is no sign today of Lisette's dangerous smile. She's entirely pleasant, the mask returned to its place. "No. I was only thinking with my brush."

"Oh? What startling thoughts you have." She smells of tea and caramel when she presses close behind Nora. She lays a hand on Nora's shoulder, and that small thing is louder than the storm. "Is that from the garden?"

"I suppose it is. I hadn't been paying attention, to tell the truth." Nora leans back—an old habit for assessing her work better. It brings her into the warm, soft press of Lisette's chest, and Lisette catches her about the waist before she can flinch away.

"I like it. I like the roses," she whispers.

Nora has painted a sketch of the strange, rose-covered creature, with its patient, shadowed eye. If she had stopped to think about it, she might have agonised about those gloomy, layered leaves and the overwhelming green of it all. She usually tries to avoid green. Troublesome colour.

"Fitting for the weather, too," Lisette adds. She unwinds from Nora and drifts over to the sofa, letting her shawl fall to the floor as she does. "Since Toby and I are sure half those garden statues are fantastical depictions of stormbeasts."

"Are they really?" Nora considers her painting once more. She's painted from memory, and she's sure she's invented half of it from imagination, but perhaps one *could* be convinced there is something dangerous and wicked beneath all that ivy. "How strange."

"This is a strange place. I prefer Esk, but Toby loves it here. His heart is here." She sighs herself down across the sofa.

"Were you born here?"

"No. Toby was. His is the main family line, you know. I'm just the poor cousin."

Nora laughs, then bites it back. "You may be poor in some aspects, Lacemont, but wealth is not one of them."

She likes the sharp cut of Lisette's smile. It's very different from her parlour look. "And what aspects might those be? If you were to observe them *honestly*?"

"You are not obliging."

A small huff escapes her lips. Laughter, perhaps. "I should think I've indulged you plenty. Did I not invite you into my home?"

"Toby's home."

Another laugh. Nora enjoys collecting them.

"I've sat here for you, hour after hour. I am here to sit for you again, if you wish. If you deem me captivating enough, of course."

Ah, so she is still sore over last night. Nora pulls out a piece of paper, considering Lisette half-sunk in shadow. "Come sit closer, near the lantern."

Lisette comes, but she doesn't bring one of the pretty little stools or the low chair. She scoops up a cushion from the sofa and drops it on the floor. And then she sits there. At Nora's feet. The stool Nora is perched on suddenly seems a dizzying height away. Lisette smiles up at her, and her mouth is all shadows and storm light.

"Like this?"

Nora wets her lips. "Yes,' she manages. "Like that is—" She breaks off. *Captivating,* she doesn't say.

Lisette's amusement deepens. "Fine?"

"No," breathes Nora. "No. It's perfect."

"Well, I'm not so sure I'd claim *perfection.*" She near preens as she says it, though, her satisfaction clear in her brown eyes. She glances up, lashes long and dark. "Not yet, in any case."

"Striving for it, are you?"

"In some fashion. Aren't we all?"

"I'd settle for something above middling," Nora mutters. She brushes in the rough shape of Lisette, the draping jacket— green, again—making a soft bundle of her. The flash of her cream trousers is pleasing, too, contrasting against the dark rug of the floor.

"Who called you middling?"

"My friends."

"You have poor friends. My friends have said nicer things about you."

"I have honest friends," corrects Nora. "Did you not call my paintings lifeless only yesterday?"

The faint touch of pink on Lisette's cheeks is lovely, and Nora rushes to capture it. "That was very rude of me."

"It was honest." She twists her brush to mark the curl of hair that tumbles across Lisette's brow. It's the same motion she might use to twine it about her finger. "You were right, and so were they. It's only that I don't know how to paint any other way."

The shadows shift again, sent changing by the storm, and she races to catch the way they weave into Lisette's hair and make thatch work of it. For a long while after, there is nothing but the painting. Even Lisette disappears into shadow and light.

"You do know." Lisette's voice is shattering. "You're doing it now."

Nora blinks, pulled away from her painting-fugue. Suddenly Lisette is no longer shadow and edge and shape, but flesh and blood and those lovely, challenging eyes are bright on her. She is sitting there, gazing up at her, and then her gaze slides past her, to her easel.

It's a good painting, even if it is still only the barest brushings of an idea. The sparse, strong brushstrokes are unmistakably *Lisette*. She can't say why, only that the brushstroke here could never be anything other than the beautiful slope of Lisette's neck, and the smudge of paint there would never be mistaken for anything other than Lisette's gentle palm.

"I barely have a face," Lisette observes.

"I've barely been painting a half-hour."

"Well, hurry up and make me whole. My leg is falling asleep."

Nora takes her time loading up her brush with paint. The problem with painting Lisette's face is that she has to look at Lisette's face. That's well and fine when Lisette is half a room away with an easel between them. It's another thing entirely when she's sitting at Nora's feet, close enough that Nora might shift her foot and rest it on Lisette's knee.

What would she do if Nora took such a liberty?

"What are you thinking when you study me so intently?" Lisette asks, her voice raw with curiosity.

Heat crawls up Nora's neck. "Value scales," she says, seizing on the closest lie.

"Like a musical scale?"

"Something like it, I suppose. Only instead of sound, it's light and shadow."

"And am I more shadow or more light?"

"Today? Everything is shadow. But in the sunlight, you are radiant." She doesn't think as the words tumble from her mouth. She's only admiring the way the shadows of Lisette's hair kiss her eyelashes. And then she sees Lisette's eyes widen, and her words flip back through her head. She fumbles her brush, almost drops it.

"Nora—"

"You have a very fine complexion," she hurries to say. "Any painter would think so."

Lisette's cheek twitches, her jaw going stiff. "I don't care what *any* painter thinks—"

"I know that. Your patchy commission record shows that just fine."

Lisette looks to the ceiling, as if the answer to her exasperations lies in the storming heavens. "It's not patchy. It's particular."

"Picky."

"Gods, you are such—"

Nora does not find out what she is, because a knock cracks right through their conversation.

"Up, up!" Felix pokes his head around the door. "Rehearsals are beginning."

Lisette gives him a very uncharacteristic gesture. "Can you not see we're busy?"

"You look very busy," he says, pleasantly. "Get off your arse and come entertain your guests."

"It seems I will remain faceless," Lisette says with great drama, and unfolds herself.

Nora takes a short breath, oddly relieved. Her sketch is the most abstract, unskilled attempt at a portrait she's done in all her time since art school, and yet she is loath to add more to it. She rather likes it.

"Go on," she says. She unclips the sketch and lays it out on the drying table with her other work. It *is* a good sketch. Better than most of her portraits to date, in fact. Even without a face.

"Go on?" Felix is there, standing over her. "No, dear Nora. You are coming too."

Nora barely gets her brush wiped down before Felix is pushing her out of the room. "I don't think I'm needed for the play," she says, but it does no good.

"I think you are quite vital," Lisette says, linking her arm into Felix's. "You can't quit now."

"Enough dallying," adds Felix. "Our masterpiece awaits!"

They make a good pair, stalking off into the storm shadows. Tall and forbidding, the both of them. She can see them on a stage, lit with aetherlight while an orchestra plays some mournful, pining dirge.

Then thunder crashes and she hurries after them, unwilling to be left alone in the dark.

Chapter Thirteen

Nora has never had any skill at social niceties, and she's starting to think she hasn't any skill at acting, either. Perhaps they're one and the same, in the end. The only grace is that, unlike her rudeness at society parties, no one here seems to mind her poor attempts at playing a wilting damsel.

Felix has supplied them all with wine again, as if hoping might make the farce easier. It does, because she's almost enjoying the chaos of it. She stands on her mark and watches Felix choreograph the battle between the adventurers and the beast. Lisette leaps onto a tea table as if she is standing on a precipice. Kalliope falls to a beast, dying dramatically across the parlour rug. Clare sinks to her death in the ocean waves, or rather, disappears behind the sofa with a blue blanket tossed over her. It doesn't do much to muffle her giggles. Finally Lisette strikes down the beast-Felix with a sword of rolled-up paper and seems to enjoy it far too much.

Tyne calls out directions, his glee turning him louder than the storm.

"Up, up, Nora," he says, chivvying her to her feet. He throws a piece of lace over her head.

She steps up, the paper in her hand. Despite the enthusiasm of the other players, she cannot match them in energy. She stumbles through her lines, unwilling to look Lisette in the eyes.

Lisette's hand is hearth-warm in her hand, soft as cream, just as it had been in the storm. Nora fixes her eyes on her paper. Page nine. Page ten. The words fall from Lisette's lips, curved in a half-smile that Nora knows is not her, but her character. *The night is ours. Sweeter than I found you.*

They are lines in a play, and not even a very good play, and still Nora's shaky heart skips. She misses a line, perhaps, because Lisette prompts her, repeating her line.

She blinks at the paper. "*Here, under the stars,*" she says, cheeks burning. What sort of line is that? Is Tyne not supposed to be a passably good playwright?

And then Tyne calls out, "And kiss."

Lisette places her palm on Nora's cheek. A butterfly touch, a brush of fingers down her jaw. Lisette's gaze drags from Nora's eyes to her mouth. She feels the heat of that glance all through her. The night is spinning away from her, far out of her control. Kiss? Here? In front of others? Oh, how she wants to be back by her easel with nothing but her paints and her brushes.

Well, that is what her thoughts think. What her heart is reaching for is quite different.

"How does one stage kiss?" she whispers, so low only Lisette hears.

Lisette smiles, and the challenge is back in her face. "Why would we stage kiss?"

And then her lips are against Nora's.

Her mouth is sweeter even than the wine. Nora turns statue-like, frozen like the creatures trapped beneath the ivy. Her blood has forgotten how to flow. Her heart has forgotten how to beat. Then Lisette pulls back, and the world floods in, shattering around her with the crash of thunder.

Nora mourns the loss of her. She grabs her, pulling her back to her mouth, and Lisette gives a shaky breath that turns Nora's thoughts to bright, brilliant vermilion. When Lisette kisses her again, she kisses like an argument. Nora cannot find a way to return her own measure, and so she surrenders, sinking into Lisette's arms.

And then there is applause.

Nora wrenches herself away, face aflame.

"Very believable," says Felix, which gets him a face full of cushion from Clare.

Nora is already stumbling back, holding Lisette at arm's length. "Pardon me," she says, faint as a whisper. "I think I'm done here."

And then she turns and flees.

⁂

The storm lashes against the house, stripes the hall in bruising stains of darkness. Nora's room is on the lee-side and so when she crawls onto the window seat and cracks the window, the air comes in as still and cold as barrow-breath.

The roses, the forest, the statues, the river, all of it gone in the rain. It is as if the world has ceased to exist, only she knows it is still there, through the veil of the storm. Somewhere through that fury there is the train, and the glow of its aether-lit carriages, and the tracks leading steadily and calmly back to Esk.

Gods, how she wishes she were back in Esk.

The door creaks. She's not even all that surprised when Lisette climbs into the window seat beside her. She's thrown off her dashing coat, and her chemise is unlaced at the collar.

"Nora," she says, low and coaxing. "I am sorry. I shouldn't have kissed you like that."

"Then I should not have kissed you either."

"No, don't say that." Lisette tucks her knees under her chin. It's such a strange, childish pose from a woman who is usually so elegant, so refined in her repose. "I liked that bit."

Nora watches Lisette's reflection in the angled window-pane. Her face is as lovely as it ever is, but the reflection is eerie and ghost-like against the storming of the skies. She shuts the window, banishing the ghost, and the window seat seems smaller again. Warm and close.

"I didn't come here to play parlour games and put on plays," she says, curling her fingers into her skirt. "I came here to paint you. Nothing has gone right for the last two years, and I need something to go right. I need *this* to go right, or I think I'll stop believing anything can."

"Nora—"

"It was foolish of me to wager that I'd be able to paint you, that I'd be able to get that painting accepted into the Annual. I know I'm not worthy of those things, not you and not the Annual. But I was too stubborn to admit it, and now I'm going to be the laughingstock of every painter in Esk."

"You won't," Lisette says. "I'd never let it be so."

"Wouldn't you? Pink dress, blue dress, hair up, hair down. You are a trial, Lisette Lacemont. Ever since you walked out of my studio—" She breaks off. "I'm not saying it's because of you, but it started there. That's the line between my life as a naive painter, thinking a bit of hard work and easy talent would get me where I wanted to be, and my life now, where I know I haven't near enough talent for hard work to get me anywhere."

"I walked out of your studio," Lisette repeats, soft. "And then what happened?"

"I burned your painting. Perhaps I brought the ill wishes of the muses down upon myself by rejecting what they had given me. Or perhaps it was only that I stopped thinking I was any good at what I did." She sinks her face into her palms, so the next words come muffled. "It wasn't good enough for you."

The silence is muffled. Nora presses her hands harder against her face, as if she can block the whole world out. She doesn't want to hear what Lisette has to say to her. When Lisette speaks, it is soft.

"I didn't think of your feelings for a moment. You looked at me like I had something to offer you, but you painted me like I was a chore. I thought you bored with me. I paid what I owed and ran away from what I thought was my own failure to captivate." Her voice twists, wry. "How selfish of me."

"It doesn't make it better to know you were only thinking of yourself."

"Darling Nora, I am only ever thinking of myself." She leans her head back against the window frame, but her gaze is unflinching. "Even tonight, I only thought of myself. I kissed you because I thought it would be delightful to have your mouth under mine. I was right, by the way." A small, dangerous smile. "I've been watching that mouth of yours. Do you know you catch your lip when you're thinking? You think quite a lot when you paint me. Oh, but I've wondered so badly what you're thinking about. It's probably very dull, isn't it? Angles and lines. Values."

Nora can't help the way her mouth twitches. "Entirely," she says, but she thinks her smile betrays her lie.

"I liked the stone creature you painted," continues Lisette. "You paint so many interesting things when you let yourself. Why do you never let yourself be interesting?" Lisette is a hand span away, and all the coldness of the storm is nothing against the warmth in her brown eyes.

"I don't wish to be interesting. I don't want people to see me. I wish they'd only see my paintings and leave me alone."

"How can they see your paintings without seeing you?" Lisette leans forwards, like she's won a point in a card game. "You must be brave."

"Braver than you? You don't let anyone see you, either."

Lisette's mouth falls open. It's an ink-dash of offence. "Me?"

"You act through life like it's a play. Like that awful play in the parlour, like it's all a game. I've been waiting for you to stop playing, but you never do, do you?"

"Why should I? Perhaps we are scared of the same thing,

you and I. I'd hate to be seen and known, and still be found wanting."

"It's inevitable."

"I wouldn't survive it."

"You would," Nora says, and the words come out bruised. "You would. I did."

Even the water drips seem to pause, so complete is the silence of that moment. Lisette's beautiful eyes go wide, fraught.

"I gave you the best of my skill, and you found me wanting. I gave my friends the best of my joy, and they found me wanting. I gave my lover the best of my heart, and she found me wanting." The truths are bitter and hard, and yet less bitter than she remembers. "I survived. I'm here."

"Yes," Lisette breathes. "Here you are."

Nora startles when Lisette touches her fingertips to Nora's cheek. Slides them down to rest at the corner of her mouth.

"And you are wrong. It's not that I found you wanting. It's that I failed to notice what I had in front of me." Her gaze drops, too, to Nora's mouth. "And I see you now. Gods, I see nothing *but* you."

A flash of lightning floods the room in stark white, and Nora topples to her feet, putting a pace between them. "I'm tired," she says, because she can't deal with Lisette's soft mouth again tonight. Not until she knows she means it.

Lisette's brows dip, gathering shadow, but her sigh is gentle. She stands, and it seems she takes half the warmth in the air with her. "Very well. I'll wish you a good night, then." She hesitates in the doorway. "You don't have to do the play if you hate it so much, Nora. I never meant to torment you."

And then she's gone. Nora closes the door and slumps against it, her forehead against the wood. Torment her? Which did she mean? The nightmare behaviour at the sittings? The play? The kiss? All?

She can't go falling in love with Lisette Lacemont. She is a known trifler. She has never been serious about a single thing in her life, by her own admission. How many times can Nora lose her heart to the same woman? Once was bad enough. Two would be devastating.

Is devastating.

Chapter Fourteen

She sleeps badly again that night. She can't even blame the storm, because it dies long before dawn. The silver light and storm-pressure vanish, leaving mud and a grey rain that is soft and endless, whispering at her windows. She pulls the drapes shut, hoping to muffle the sound.

It doesn't work. It chases her into her dreams, stalking her through her uneasy sleep-wanderings. She dreams of roses choking her, growing through her mouth and down her throat. She dreams of fey, stone creatures stalking after her, melting through the shadows, and when she turns, they leap upon her.

She wakes with a hitched breath. Her throat burns, dry with thirst, and all the air smells of rain. The curtains drift inwards, dark shadows in the dim glow of veiled moonlight. She rolls to her feet, padding across the carpet to drag the drapes aside. The window is flung open, the night pouring in. The carpet beneath her bare feet is damp with rain, and dark with mud.

She slams the window shut. The wind must be stronger than she thought, to pry her window open. Surely she had closed it the night before. She flicks through her memory and remembers closing the window, banishing Lisette's ghost-reflection. Remembers the way that space had been filled with Lisette's body, folded in with her like the seat had been made for cradling them, and them alone.

When she enters the breakfast room, Lisette is holding court with Felix and Tyne. Clare is reading a book and ignoring their antics, and Nora slips into the seat beside her, entirely unnoticed.

Almost entirely. She's watching Lisette's reflection in the curved side of the silver teapot, and so she catches the wisp of a look that Lisette gives her. Nora feels it like a brush of a hand on her cheek, like lips against her own.

Not a dream, not a night-dark fantasy she'd summoned from her own wantings, but a memory still sweet with wine. Lisette Lacemont had kissed her.

Beyond the teapot, the aftermath of the storm is strewn beyond the window. The mud slick of the garden smears into mist, disappearing into the sullen skies. And what isn't mud is water. In the grey light, islands of roses jut from a murky, glistening ocean. The manor might as well have been cut adrift in the night, left to float away from the world.

"We're flooded in," Tyne says, with a grim pronouncement better suited to a stage tragedy. "The road is sunk well and truly. Don't think we'd be going anywhere for a few days."

The glass door of the breakfast room screeches, pushed inwards, and they all startle. It's only Toby, wet to the knees with mud.

"Cursed gods, Tobes," Lisette says, striding over to him. "You went wandering?"

"I wasn't empty-handed," he says, and hauls himself through the door, mud and all. He has a crossbow. It's an ancient thing, surely as old as the manor itself, and the arrow tips are cruel, tipped with hooked aetherglass.

"I wouldn't trust that thing to protect against a weasel, let alone a stormbeast." Lisette slams the door shut. "What's the news, then?"

"Nothing amiss in the farm cottages. Some sheep unaccounted for, but that could as easily be the storm as a beast. Guards came down from Esk on the train this morning, and there's been a hunting party formed. Storm made landfall over by Stote." He crouches by the hearth and feeds a few more logs in. Despite the overbearing heat, it's necessary to have them burning. Everything would be far too damp without it. "It's flooded deep in parts. If you have to go outside, be careful."

"No one is going outside," Lisette declares. "Honestly, Toby. The mud alone would stop anyone sensible. I propose we set up for parlour games upstairs."

Nora can't stand the thought of another day spent in the parlour, trying not to stare at Lisette's mouth. In fact, she deems it entirely impossible. She has no idea how she's going to last through being trapped here together. She'll need a blessing from the muses themselves to get her thoughts back to painting again.

If Toby deems it safe, she wants to be outdoors. Quiet, crisp air, and no chance of parlour games. She puts aside her finished breakfast plate and gets to her feet. "Is the way to the well clear, Toby?"

Toby scrunches his mouth thoughtfully. "Yes, I reckon so. Wanting to make a wish? Hey, outside with that, Bess."

Bess freezes in the open door, muddy all through. She has a thick branch in her jaws. Nora takes it and tosses it a short way into a puddle, and Bess throws herself after it in delight.

She wipes her muddy hand on her trousers. A wish is exactly what she needs. "I thought I shouldn't miss the chance. Not while I'm here."

A chair scrapes, Lisette leaping to her feet. "Wait a moment, I want to come, too."

Toby sighs, but waits by the door for the two of them to run and fetch their coats. Nora returns to the breakfast room to find the rest with their coats, too.

She has the distinct feeling that she's started something. "I thought no one was going outside."

"You decided we were," Felix says, quite breezily. "Where one goes—"

"All go!" the rest cheer.

"Even if you are abandoning our play," he adds, and Tyne shakes his head with all the drama of the theatre.

They traipse outside. The morning light is dim, barely bright enough to make their path clear. She steps down into the puddled waters of the flooded kitchen garden, her boots soaked through in a moment. Clare makes a sound of disgust as she follows. Toby leading, they wade forwards, and the chime-like sound of their passage is the only disturbance in the stillness.

A single sigh of wind ripples the drowned roses as they spill into the courtyard. The water is bitter as midwinter, seeping through her stockings and turning her toes to ice. The roses are bedraggled from the storm, torn through and bereft of flowers. Dark water pools in all the hollows and shadows, and the well brims over with it. It trickles over the stone lip and down the sides, as if the well is the heart of the flood, ever-flowing.

Nora digs a coin from her pocket and wades forwards. The glass-clear water shivers as she nears, and she lets the coin drop from her fingers. It falls fast, glinting gold once, and then it is gone down into the depths.

"Bravery," she whispers. The wind gusts, and the water ripples. She thinks of her wager, and the Annual, and the particular anguish of capturing Lisette Lacemont in paint. She cannot do it. Any painting that wins over the Annual will not be the painting Lisette has asked her to make. "I wish for bravery to see things through to the end, even if it isn't the end I sought."

Another gust of wind. The copper cup chimes up in the roof-peak of the well-house.

"Hm," says Toby. "Best do as it asks."

She hopes her face conveys how she feels about a well thinking anything, but she takes the cup. She needn't winch it, not with the water so high. She merely leans over and fills the cup.

Then she drinks, and the water is cold enough to hurt, searing through her. But it doesn't turn her to ice, like she thinks it might. It fills her with the sky, fresh and clean, and it seems like every last cobweb on her thoughts has been washed away. All the dried paint and bent bristles, finally gone. All the stiffness, lifelessness, muddiness.

"Me too," says Felix, so close to her ear that she startles and drops the cup. He catches it, right before it hits the water, and gives her a sheepish look. "Sorry."

"No," she says, and smiles. "Good catch."

He stares at her, and then the rest of them are there, clamouring for their turn at tasting the storm-blessed water. She steps away and gives them room. They'd make a lovely painting, gathered around the well, clutching at each other and laughing. She's so focused on trying to organise the painting in her mind she doesn't realise Lisette is not with them until Lisette is there, taking up all her sight.

"Bravery?" she says. Her hair sticks to her cheeks, damp with the misting rain. It's left her crowned in silver.

"Eavesdropping, were you?"

"I'm nosy." She leans in, one hand sliding up Nora's back.

Her thoughts drift in a delightful way, and then she's thinking of vermilion mixing with all her paints and tinting the world warm and rose-kissed. She really shouldn't be wanting to kiss Lisette here. Even if she suspects Lisette is quite sincere, after all, in all the ways she teases and taunts her.

"Wait," she says, pushing a hand against Lisette's chest. Oh, awful choice. Her chest is soft, delightfully so, and her thoughts scatter. "No."

"No?" Lisette pulls back. "Why *no*?"

"Because I am painting you," Nora says, gathering her senses back, frayed as they are. "I cannot kiss a subject! It's...unprofessional."

Lisette laughs. "Unprofessional? I'm not even paying you."

"Gods, I'd hope not." Nora untangles herself from Lisette's arms. "Let me finish painting you first."

"Are you really going to make me wait until the cursed painting is finished before I can kiss you again?"

"If you might play nicely with me, it'll be finished faster."

"Dearest," Lisette says, "It had better be the swiftest painting you ever make."

Then Bess leaps between them, dripping and muddy, bringing a stick for Nora to throw. She catches Toby laughing. At her, no doubt. Somehow, she doesn't mind that like she used to.

When she makes it back to her painting room, she flings the windows wide onto the drowned gardens. The view is grey and mud and nothing but a few valiant rose bushes poking from the waters. She paints them, a gathering of scratchy brush marks against the silken greys. Her Esk friends would laugh to see her shape the impression of stalks and leaves so tenderly. The wild uncaring of the storm-flung landscape captivates her, though. Both the fury of the previous night, and this endless trudge of weather, too. She's always known storms from the solid, ancient grasp of Esk's stone buildings and streets, and even the annual floods of the river are a known and predictable thing.

Storms rarely hit Esk with the fury that had crashed over the manor. Nora has never known anything like it, and so she paints the mist and grey skies and grey water, the endless expanse of it. The world looks as adrift and lost as she had felt when she had first arrived.

The manor had been a stranger, with its shadows and creaks and wild, untamed garden, and somehow she has become a stranger in it, too. A person who paints strange, dreamlike landscapes, and who kisses beautiful, rakish women, and who stares down storms and tries to paint them.

It splits her right down the middle, the sudden realisation of it. A lightning strike of a realisation, as silver and sharp as storm aether. She pulls out the large canvas, the one she had been saving for another sitting with Lisette, and it's barely settled on the easel before she is painting.

There's a lot of colour in silver, she knows. Lilac and cornflower and lapis. Umber, ochre, and even troublesome green. The colours dance against one another as she lays down paint as thick as the mist outside, and she fancies she might be painting with the mist itself.

It's not a landscape, exactly. The land is a mere sliver of shadow anchoring her canvas, and all the rest, as high as her arm can reach, is the storm. The clouds seethe at her command, spilling forwards with such force that when she stands back, aching and exhausted in the late hours of the evening, they seem to spill out of the canvas itself.

The dinner bell rings, then rings again, more chaotically. There's laughter, and the ringing shuts off abruptly. Nora pulls herself back into the present and considers her painting again, this time more critically.

It is the work of a stranger. It doesn't look like anything she's painted before.

She finds the little square of linen canvas with her stone creature and props it near her giant storm. Then the faceless sketch of Lisette, all tumbled, gestural lines. And her first attempt at the storm, angry and jarring.

Yes, there is the trail. Like a line of footprints, she can trace her journey from one canvas into another. Emlyn had been right. She *has* been painting middling things, but she isn't now. Not anymore. Gods, is this how he feels with everything he paints?

She feels as large as her storm.

Chapter Fifteen

Painting a storm is one thing. Painting Lisette Lacemont is another beast entirely. Nora has been lying on her bed, staring at the ceiling and contemplating the fact that despite everything she has worked towards, she may very well not be a portrait painter at all. Is it better to be a painter of trite landscapes than a painter of lifeless portraits?

No, she is being ungenerous. She knows landscapes can be wild, enchanting things. She's stood, locked in awe, over Emlyn's paintings enough times. But even Emlyn can never get his paintings into the Annual, and he is a better painter than her by far. It's easy to admit that truth to herself here, away from his smug face.

Nora doesn't tell a soul about her painting. It sits on her easel, unknown, and she drifts through the rest of the day in something like a dream. The soft victory fades to gentle worry. Can she do it again? Is it enough?

After dinner, she is funnelled to the parlour, where she

finds Toby sitting captive on the sofa, Bess across his lap. Bess wags her tail as Nora takes her seat.

"Ah," Toby says, giving her a sideways look. "I see you escaped the cast list in the end."

"Only to be caught in the audience," she says, and he laughs.

Then Clare shushes them, and the aetherlights all go dark, except for the one in Lisette's hand. And the play begins.

It is, quite frankly, a disaster, in the way that only a barely-learned play by a troupe of half-tipped friends can be. Nora shields her face with her hands as Kalliope forgets her cues, and Lisette forgets half her lines, and Felix knocks over the backing curtain and takes out her lantern. Clare hits the ground far too hard in her death scene and swears like a ferryman. Tyne is laughing too hard at Lisette's dramatics to play the part of the love-stricken damsel with any veracity.

Despite this, Felix is still a terrifying beast, stalking Lisette so convincingly that Bess rouses to defend her, sinking her teeth into the fur coat with a furious growl. He has to unmask to get her to leave off, and Lisette breaks character to kiss Bess' dear head. Or maybe she doesn't. Maybe all of her Starling antics are merely Lisette letting herself have fun. Maybe, for once, she isn't acting at all. Lisette plays, but she never does a thing she doesn't want. Everything she does, she does because she wants to.

Even this play, this ridiculous farce with her friends. It doesn't matter that they've left half the lines out. It doesn't matter that the fight scene went awry, and the companions departed in the wrong order. It doesn't matter that they're laughing harder than their audience, and it doesn't matter that Bess has become the hero of the tale, not Lisette at all.

The performance ends with Tyne and Lisette clutching at each other in great dramatics. And Nora learns what a stage kiss looks like.

Felix leans over the back of the sofa and whispers, "Yours was much better."

Then Toby is clapping, solemn and grave, and everyone cheers, and Nora joins in the applause as Lisette and Tyne make their bows.

"It was a frightful mess," Tyne says, delighted. "Good work, everyone."

Toby whistles Bess back to his side before she can get too roused into chaos by the uproar. "You lot better put that all back in the attic before you head back to town."

"Yes, yes, you bore," Lisette says. "Don't say we didn't entertain you."

"You never fail to bring me entertainments, dear cousin," he says, sounding entirely tired and fond. "Now, off to bed with all of us. There'll be clear up to do in the gardens tomorrow, and I expect you all to be helping."

This is, strangely enough, greeted with another wine-tipped cheer. Nora shuffles off with the others, and before she disappears into her rooms, she glimpses Lisette at the end of the hall, watching her. Waiting, perhaps, to see if Nora will hold her door open for her.

She shuts it.

The good mood of the play lingers, but not forever. She dresses for bed, combs out her hair and plaits it. Washes her hands and face with cold, scented water. The whole time she is thinking of Lisette throwing the cape over her lovely shoulders. Cupping her face. Kissing her.

Felix had been right. Their kiss *had* been better.

It would be better again, she thinks, if she could kiss her truly. A proper kiss. Not a stage play, not a flirtation, not a tease. If she could kiss Lisette the way she paints, if she could trace the curves of her, changing the shape of her with a touch.

The night is whittled away by the rattle of her window, and the ticking of the clock in the hall, and Nora's own heated thoughts. There is only one thing that helps when she is as restless as this.

She pulls on her dressing gown and heads to her painting room. The floor is cold through her socked feet as she approaches, and she's concentrating on being silent, and so she doesn't notice the glow of golden light from beneath the door until she gets there. The door is ajar, and when she rests her hand lightly against it, it swings in. Easy, without a sound.

Lisette is standing in front of the easel, staring at the storm.

Nora stops in the doorway, caught fast. Lisette's nightgown trails on the ground, falling from her shoulders in deep pleats, and her hair is down, falling in autumn ripples down her back. Nora wants to sink her hands in it.

She must make some sort of noise, because Lisette turns.

"Oh," she says, and smiles. "I couldn't sleep."

"Neither could I," Nora says. She closes the door behind her. "I thought I'd come paint."

"Does that help the sleeplessness?"

"Sometimes."

"Perhaps it's worth a try, then." She looks back to the

canvas. "It's beautiful. It's a bit terrifying." She hovers a hand over the wet oils, on Nora's signature etched in the lower corner. "You finished it."

"Not a scrap of canvas left uncovered," she says, coming to stand beside Lisette. Because she can't help it, she pushes her hand away from the canvas. It makes her nervous, seeing hands so close to the wet paint.

Lisette twists her hand, catching Nora's wrist. She tugs her hand up between them. Nora's sleeve falls back, revealing her arm right up to the elbow. The night air is odd against her bare skin, and Lisette's gaze tracks down her wrist, down her arm. She trails her fingers down, raising aches right along Nora's skin. "Paint me," she says, low.

Nora swallows. "I'll try."

"No different from the storm." She changes direction, running those fingers along Nora's cheek. "No different from the roses."

Nora watches, anchored, as Lisette pushes her hair back over her shoulders. Tugs at the ribbons at the neck of her nightgown until the collar falls slack, open, and reveals the gentle shadows of her collarbones and the pale skin dipping down.

Is Nora supposed to paint her in her nightdress, with her collar open so? What sort of scandal would she cause, presenting such a thing? And then Lisette undoes a button, and another, and then, with a whisper, her nightdress falls to the floor.

She is entirely bare, in nothing but her undressed hair.

"It's no different, Nora," she says.

She settles on the sofa like that, all silk-soft skin and rain-dark hair, and Nora kneels beside her.

"May I?" she asks, hands hovering.

Lisette's smile is all shadows. "Put me where you wish to have me."

Even Nora cannot misunderstand her meaning. She knows she is blushing, but she hardly thinks she should be ashamed of it. Anyone would, when faced with what she is facing.

Lisette's skin is warm beneath her palms. She spills her across the silks and cushions, tugging her until she melts amongst it. "Like that," she says, at last, skimming her fingers across the softness of Lisette's thigh. "Exactly like that."

When she reaches for her brushes, she is calm. When she looks at Lisette, she feels the steady burn of the painting catching fire within her. She paints fast, too aware of the night chill on Lisette's bare skin, though Lisette doesn't show any discomfort. Her eyes have fallen shut, as if she has found some sleep there, amongst all the silks.

She isn't asleep, though. Now and then, Nora looks up to see her eyes open, her gaze on Nora. She is watching Nora as keenly as Nora watches her.

Like the storm, there are more colours to Lisette than Nora expected. Like the storm, she takes shape with expressive, bold marks that Nora hardly feels she is controlling. The curve of her hip. The tangles of her hair. All laid in with a twist of her wrist, or twitch of her fingers.

Then the slope of Lisette's dark brows. The mole on her cheek. The distracting fullness of her mouth. The tease of those dark lashes. That dash of vermilion she's been longing after. Cheek. Lips.

When she steps back, her heart thuds in her chest. It is a finished painting.

It is nothing she can submit to the annual.

"Nora?" Lisette is unmoved, still spilled across the silks, but she is watching with tension right through her. "How did it come along?"

Nora places her brush aside and wipes her hands on a rag out of habit. There's hardly any need. She hasn't got a speck of paint on her. "Magnificently, I think. It'll take the morning light to know for sure."

"And have I a face?"

She laughs. "You have a face. And a lovely one, too."

Lisette's smile is slow and pleased. "Then come here." She sits, her arms held out for Nora, and when Nora comes, she tugs at the buttons of her nightgown, opening her collar. She slides her hand inside, cupping the crook of Nora's neck. "You have painted me now."

"I have."

"And it is finished."

"I believe it is."

Lisette's gaze drops, her thumb resting over Nora's pulse. She smiles. "Then why aren't you kissing me?"

Nora does. She kisses her, and then she is being kissed. No, she is being devoured. Lisette kisses her with hunger—thirst—like Nora is the last thing left for her to cling to in a vast sea. Kisses the corner of her mouth, and then tugs Nora's collar aside and kisses the soft shadow under her jaw, and over the flutter of her pulse, and drags her teeth to the base of her neck and bites, gently and maddeningly, as if she wants to leave a mark.

Nora falls beneath her, because what else is there to wish to do?

"So lovely," Lisette murmurs, gathering Nora's hands in her own. She presses a kiss to her knuckles, and then turns her hand over and kisses her palm. "Such skilled hands. They've worked so hard." Kisses her wrist. "Let them rest, now."

She pins Nora's hands above her head, both gathered in one firm grip. Nora might break it if she wished to stop, but she doesn't wish to. Not when Lisette presses her body over Nora's, her other hand sliding up Nora's thigh, hiking her nightgown up higher and higher.

No, she doesn't wish to stop at all.

Chapter Sixteen

Felix lets out a low breath, the sound catching in his teeth. He steps back, then back again, then throws his hands in the air in triumph. "She's done it," he declares. His grin is wide. "She finished the painting, and *what a painting.*"

Nora waits for someone to shove him, or tell him to stop being dramatic, but Lisette's gathering of friends only nod, all gazes fixed to her easel. Lisette tips her chin in a pleased manner, giving Nora that look she has, a mix of amusement and victory. She's awfully pleased for a woman who currently has her entire set of friends staring at her naked body.

Even if it's only a painted version, and all the most interesting bits are covered.

"It's entirely troubling," Clare says, soft. She smiles at Nora. "It's certainly beautiful, but you've captured that awful challenge of Lisette. She rather dares one to come closer while promising to devour them if they do. You want to do nothing but stare, but feel compelled to drop your gaze."

"I've never seen a more honest picture of Lise," says Toby.

He'd taken one look at the painting, long enough to realise his beloved cousin was nude, and had promptly gone to stand behind the easel. "And I don't mean the part where she's unclothed."

"No, I quite know what you mean," Kalliope adds. "It's precisely the Lisette we know and love."

It is, because it is the Lisette that Nora has come to know, too. Beneath all the barbs and silks and flighty disdain is a person who challenged her to reach higher than she had dared to reach before. She'd broken everything Nora had held close, every misplaced thought and crushing belief. She'd set Nora free.

"Whatever are you going to do with it?" Felix asks.

"I'll display it at my townhouse. In the parlour, perhaps." Lisette's smile is sharp as glass. "No one will fail to notice it."

The laughter is bright and shocked, rising to the old beams of the ceiling. Clare waves her hands at Lisette, aghast, but Felix looks like he's already planning the scandal-piece for the papers.

"You'll be a notable for sure, when the Season comes," Kalliope says, coming to stand beside Nora. "I look forward to seeing you at the evening parties."

"How do you make that out?"

"You painted Lisette Lacemont. And entirely scandalously, too. If that doesn't put you at the heart of goings-on, I don't know what will."

A notable. She doesn't know what to do with that. She'll have commissions again by the handful, though by rights, her commission book will be in Emlyn's hands.

She won't be winning her wager. This painting is not

going to the Gallery Annual. Even if, through some fit of fancy, the Gallery accepted it, she'd never be able to hang this moment up for every curious face of Esk to see. This moment when Lisette had trusted her with everything.

She hopes she has done her justice. She had tried. With every twist of her wrist, every gentle drag of the brush through glistening paint, she had done her best.

The Lisette that stares out from the painting with lowered lashes and curving smile is *her* Lisette. Her infuriating, intangible Lisette, that has lured and teased and dragged her on until finally Nora had understood what it meant to paint.

Nothing else she has ever done has taught her that quite the way Lisette taught her.

"We'll see," is all she says, and Kalliope gives her a knowing look, laughter in the corner of her mouth.

Nora doesn't mind it. For once, she feels entirely in on the joke.

Chapter Seventeen

Emlyn tugs her painting stool over and sits on it with that grave dignity he shrugs into on a whim. He hasn't looked away from her painting since she unveiled it.

She leans against the wall and tips her face to the window. Her studio is an attic space, and through the dormer window, the tea-brown rooftops of Esk are steeped dark in the rain. A bedraggled wren hunches in the shelter of her window, puffed up like a fluffed tassel.

"Nora," Emlyn says, finally. He sounds... Well, he sounds delighted.

She straightens, wary. Emlyn's delight can mean all manner of trials for his friends. "Yes?"

But there is no trouble in his face as he smiles at her. He so very rarely smiles like this. It's sunlight all the way through. "You did it. I knew you could."

"Yes, Fairthorne. I can, in fact, paint. Well done."

"Before you merely pushed a brush around. But *this* is painting. It's magnificent." He leans back on the stool, balancing himself with one foot on her painting table. "How did you ever manage such a..." He trails off, flipping forwards again to squint at the canvas. "And that little sequence... With that masterful grasp of the edges? Where did you learn that?"

She looks back out the window. She'd learned it from him, though she'll never tell him so. His tragic levels of self-grandeur needed no bolstering. "Here and there."

"I've always loved your painting, you know," he says.

Nora stares fiercely out the window. Her eyes prickle with treacherous heat. "I would not have guessed it," she manages, and it comes out far softer than she means it to.

"You were endlessly frustrating, never seeing anything through to completion. I'm thrilled you figured it out. We need you, Bristles. Let's take the Annual by storm! Let's show them what painting can truly be! None of that stiff and true-to-form dreariness. We'll bring them *colour*. Emotion! We—"

"Mercy, Emlyn," she says, laughing despite herself. "Maybe next year. I'm not submitting this. You win our wager."

His mouth makes a twitch that might have almost been a pout. "Fair," he sighs. "You know I'm not actually going to steal your commission book, right? I was just trying to nettle you."

"I didn't at first. I figured it out eventually." She hops up to sit on the windowsill. "And you? Are you trying for the Annual again?"

His smile goes thoughtful. "I think I am, actually. Very well, I change the terms of our wager. Instead of passing over your commission book, you can come to the opening day of the Annual and cheer for me with all your enthusiasm."

"You're very sure they'll take you. I'll look a right goose cheering for an artist who isn't in the exhibition."

He tips his chin up. "Don't fret. I don't intend to let anyone look like a goose."

She laughs. For the first time in a long while, the thought of cheering a friend's success doesn't make her want to sink through the floor in anguish. She hopes he *does* get a painting in. She wants to be there, cheering.

A knock at the door has them both turning. A whisper of dangerously pale silk peeks around the door, and then Lisette is there. She's wearing fawn trousers and a green silk coat, her hair looped in a loose braid against the back of her neck. Nora could easily paint her like that, looking like a festival window-dressing stepped into life.

"There you are," she says, smiling. "Everyone is off for tea at Holloway's, so I hope you've nothing to keep you from joining us."

Emlyn hops to his feet. "I'm certainly not keeping anyone. I was just leaving," he says. He nods politely at Lisette as he passes her, but his gaze is on the shifting silk of her coat rather than on her face. Faces have always held very little interest to him.

"Curious man," Lisette says. "He looks familiar. Would I know him?"

"He gets around," says Nora, holding out a hand. "Tea at Holloway's? I'm hardly dressed for it."

"You're never dressed for anything." She tugs Nora to her feet, and then closer in again. "But don't let that stop you."

"Only if you promise to come back here afterwards and let me paint you. I like that coat."

Lisette rests her palm to Nora's cheek, thumb rubbing at something there. Paint, perhaps. "Oh, very well. Just for you."

Just for her. Just for them. Just the quiet of the painting studio, the soft rise-and-fall of their matching breath. The way Lisette watches Nora, the way Nora longs for Lisette through her canvas, through every brushstroke. It's like nothing else.

Nora *can* paint anything and anyone, and maybe even do it a good sight better than anyone else, but she knows that there is nothing that will ever enthral her as much as painting her Lisette.

An Extra Scene

A FEW MONTHS LATER

The Gallery Annual is the unofficial start of Esk's Wintering Season. Nora has attended once before, when Juniper's painting had won a spot on the hallowed walls. She'd spent the afternoon hunched behind a crowd of artists, sipping her drink and scowling at anyone who got too close.

She hadn't meant to scowl, really. She'd only been feeling prickly, because Juniper was so proud, and so boastful, and Nora could only think about how the Gallery had overlooked her own work completely.

She's not that person anymore. When Emlyn greets her with a wide smile, she finds her own smile is just as bright, and entirely genuine.

"It's marvellous," she says, after she sees his painting. "I'm so proud of you."

He leans back, all his face glowing. "By the muses," he says, pressing a hand to his chest. "Was that sentiment? Honest sentiment. From my Bristles?"

That has her summoning up one of her scowls, but he only laughs at her.

"We'll see one of your works here soon. I'm sure of it," he says. "Is your stunning muse around somewhere?"

"She's off chattering," Nora says.

"As must be I," he says. He's dressed in a fine shirt and coat, clearly intending to make the most of the event. "I have potential clients to charm."

"Go dazzle them," she says, shooing him off.

He goes, and he really is at risk of dazzling people, glowing with success like that. Perhaps she might know what that feels like, some day. She isn't so attached to the idea as she had been in the past, though.

It no longer feels like her sole purpose in life. Her focus has shifted.

She drifts back to Emlyn's painting to listen in on the gallery-goers' opinions of his work. Most of them are in raptures over it, and the few who are not are, in her opinion, wrong.

It really is a magnificent piece.

"Well, of course there is skill," says an older woman with a tightly-netted bun. She's got her face angled away from the painting, as if she doesn't wish to make eye contact. "But the choice of subject is concerning."

Her companion tips his nose up. "How so? The model has an unmatched stare. I've never seen anything like it."

"Well, yes. But isn't it uncomfortable, to be stared at so?"

Nora is tugged aside, and she misses the rest of the conversation. She rounds on her interloper, and grins when Lisette holds out a thin, sparkling glass of apple-spirits. "You interrupted my eavesdropping."

"And what horrid things were they saying about your dear friend this time?"

"Oh, nothing but praise for Emlyn. His poor model is getting the brunt of the criticism."

Lisette gives her a look from beneath her lashes. "And what do you think of the model?"

Nora considers Emlyn's painting. From their vantage point beside a potted fern, she has a sharp side-angle view of his masterwork, and a good view of the faces of its viewers. It really is garnering a lot of attention.

He has extended all his skill in the painting of the portrait. The model has a face like none Nora has met before, her eyes dark as midnight and piercing as ice.

Emlyn was bold to pick her as a subject. There is beauty to her, but it's nothing gentle, and nothing easy. It's hard to look at the painting for any length of time without feeling like one is under attack.

"I can't fathom why he chose to make his Annual debut with such an antagonistic painting," she says at last. "But it certainly shows his skill."

"Perhaps you should have entered my painting, after all," muses Lisette. Her fingers brush against Nora's waist. "It might not have made such a scandal with everyone distracted by that."

"I prefer its current home. It suits your parlour very well."

"My guests think so, also," Lisette says, her mouth crooking at the corner.

"You are a trial."

Lisette draws her further into the shelter of the fern. The fronds brush against Nora's cheek, soft and teasing. "I'm planning a dinner party with some of this Season's crowd," she murmurs. "You'll come, won't you?"

Nora freezes, her glass halfway to her mouth. "Oh."

"I'll invite your friends," adds Lisette. "Both of them. And Felix will be there. You adore Felix."

"Adore is a strong word."

Lisette laughs. "Please come. Come sit beside me, as mine. I want everyone to know that I am not unattached this Season."

Heat blooms across her cheeks. "Is that wise?"

"It would be the wisest thing I have ever done," Lisette says. The bright, fair daylight makes the glass beads at her throat glint and glimmer, and the reflected light kisses her neck. Pink. Lilac. Madder. "Nora?"

Nora lifts her gaze back to Lisette's face. She opens her mouth and finds herself bereft of words.

"You look entirely shocked. Don't tell me you had secretly planned to set me aside for the Season?" Lisette says, teasing. She draws her fingers lightly over the back of Nora's hand.

Nora wants to grab her. Wants to tug her in and kiss her. She can't do so here, at a public gathering. Why ever did Lisette choose now to ask her this?

"I didn't expect to be a part of your plans this Season," she admits.

"Nora, darling. My plans this Season are entirely you. I'd have you join me everywhere I go."

"No, thank you," Nora says. "I do have work to do, you know. I'm hardly about to become a socialite."

"Pity. You'd make such a pretty socialite, all idling in silks."

"I'd only get paint on them."

"You'd start a new trend."

"I'd get murdered by the collected dressmakers of Esk."

Lisette laughs, and it's as pretty as any of the artworks on the walls. She is prettier than any of the artworks. No passage of paint or charcoal or pastel will ever come close to her beauty, but the muses must know Nora is going to spend the rest of her life trying anyway.

She blinks, the force of her thought leaving her breathless.

"Why are you looking so amused?" Lisette says, wary.

"Because I just realised I've been a little foolish."

"Only now? Darling, you're behind the times."

She laughs. She can't help it. "Lisette."

"Yes?"

"I'll come to your dinner party. But you must come to one of my gatherings, too."

She arches an brow. "An artisan evening? What does that entail?"

"Social drinks and games. Poetry. Critique. Flights of fancy."

"Well, I can do the drinking and the fancying, I'm sure."

"If you are to declare yourself attached, then I must too," Nora adds, her heart beating a touch faster than it rightly should.

Lisette blinks at her, and then a delightful, faint pink darkens her cheeks. Her smile is slow and promising. "We've been here an age. Have you fulfilled the terms of your wager yet?"

Nora can't look away from Lisette's mouth. "Pardon?"

"You've cheered for your friend, you've admired his painting. We can go, can we not?"

Nora sets her glass aside. She can come back on a quieter day to admire the rest of the paintings, when there isn't such a crowd all around.

"Yes," she says. She's light as air all through. "To yours?"

"Mine," Lisette says, drawing Nora into her side with a hand pressed gently to her waist.

It's a quiet touch, but it feels as loud as a kiss.

Afterword

Thank you so much for reading this little novella. I hope it inspired and delighted you.

Join my newsletter and follow along for more cosy, queer stories set in the world of Esk.

www.theahawthorne.com/newsletter

Acknowledgments

Thank you to every dear person who stumbled upon and read my first novella, and turned around to cheer me on. I'm releasing this second one for you.

Thank you also to my partner, for believing in me on the days I doubt myself, and to my friends, for never talking me down from my dreams. I'd never have the courage without you.

About the Author

Thea Hawthorne writes queer, cosy fantasy from her home in Tasmania, Australia, always with a cup of tea close to hand. She enjoys rainy days, both in books and in real life, and will always talk about the weather. In her books, you'll find a delightful blend of found family, folklore, quiet pursuits, a lot of warmth and a little dash of steaminess.

www.theahawthorne.com